MYSTERY WEEKEND

Holly was halfway along the corridor when there was a crash and the sound of breaking glass. Suddenly the hall was full of people as guests came running from all over the house.

'Where did it come from?' shouted Mrs Partridge.

'The library, I think,' Mark said.

Miranda looked at her plan of the house. 'This way,' she said.

They made a dash for the library, falling over one another in their haste to get there. They stopped on the doorstep. There was a jagged break in one of the library windows. Lying on the floor was a brick with a piece of paper wrapped round it.

'What does it say?' Peter asked.

Mrs Partridge cleared her throat. 'It says, "I shall kill. Will it be tonight? Be on your guard!"'

Miranda gave a little scream and Holly gasped. The mystery had begun!

The Mystery Kids series

1 Spy-Catchers!
2 Lost and Found
3 Treasure Hunt
4 The Empty House
5 Smugglers Bay
6 Funny Money
7 Blackmail!
8 Mystery Weekend
9 Wrong Number
10 Hostage!
11 Box of Tricks
12 Kidnap!

Mystery Weekend

Fiona Kelly

a division of Hodder Headline plc

Special thanks to Helen Magee

Created by Ben M. Baglio
London W6 0HE

First published in Great Britain in 1996
by Hodder Children's Books

10 9 8 7 6 5 4

A Catalogue record for this book is
available from the British Library

ISBN 0 340 65565 8

Typeset by Hewer Text Composition Services, Edinburgh
Printed and bound in Great Britain by
Mackays of Chatham PLC, Chatham, Kent

Hodder Children's Books
a division of Hodder Headline plc
338 Euston Road
London NW1 3BH

Contents

The house with two names

'And keep listening for the winners of the Mystery Weekend competition,' the DJ said. 'It could be your chance to stay at Granville Towers for a weekend to solve a dastardly murder. Who are the lucky winners? Who's going to get to play detective for the weekend? Stay tuned and find out! All will be revealed right after the news.'

Holly, Peter and Miranda looked at one another as the radio station jingle played. They were huddled round Peter's radio in the little boxroom Mr Hamilton let them use as their 'office'. They had entered the competition run by the local radio station just for fun. But now that the winners were about to be announced they were really keyed up.

'I can't listen. I can't stand the suspense,'

Holly Adams said as she twisted a strand of her light brown hair nervously between her fingers.

'Don't listen then,' said Peter Hamilton. 'Stick your fingers in your ears. We'll tell you if we win.'

Holly looked at him scathingly. 'I'd hear Miranda anyway,' she said. 'Even if I wore earplugs.'

Miranda Hunt tossed her long blonde hair and plumped herself down on one of the cushions the three of them used instead of chairs. 'Just because I don't mumble,' she said.

Holly and Peter grinned. Miranda's voice was notoriously loud. She certainly didn't mumble!

'If we do win you'll be able to hear Miranda at the other end of Highgate,' Peter said to Holly.

'We'll win,' said Miranda confidently. 'After all, they don't call us the Mystery Kids for nothing.'

The three friends had got their name from a headline in the paper after they had solved their very first mystery. It had stuck ever since. The boxroom in Peter's house was their headquarters. They had a map of North London pinned to the wall and coloured pins to mark suspicious happenings in the Highgate area.

'Here,' said Peter, tossing a book to Holly. 'Read a book. Take your mind off the competition.'

'The Inside-Out Clue,' Holly said, reading the title. 'I'm too excited to read now but I don't know this one. Can I borrow it?'

The Mystery Kids loved mystery books. Their all-time favourite was *Harriet the Spy* but so long as it was a mystery story, they were eager to read. Best of all, though, they liked solving real life mysteries. There hadn't been much in the way of mysteries happening in Highgate recently and the competition to win a mystery weekend had been too good a chance to miss.

Holly looked nervously at the radio. 'What if our entry got lost in the post?' she said.

'Don't be daft,' said Peter. 'That hardly ever happens.'

'Honestly, Holly,' said Miranda. 'You aren't

usually like this. Listen to the news or something and stop worrying. We'll hear the result in a minute.'

Holly wrinkled her nose. 'It's all about politics,' she said as she listened to the announcer's voice. 'Politics is boring.'

'I'll tell you a joke then,' said Miranda.

'No,' said Peter. 'Not that, anything but that.' He stuck his head under a cushion.

Miranda grinned in delight. She wrote a bad jokes column for the lower school magazine, *The Tom-tom*. She actually *liked* the bad jokes.

Her face lit up. 'What do you get if you cross a jeep with a dog?' she said.

Holly raised her eyebrows.

'OK,' she said. 'What do you get if you cross a jeep with a dog?'

'A Land Rover,' Miranda said. She hooted with laughter.

Peter banged his head on the floor and Miranda laughed even louder. That was another thing about Miranda – the worse the joke, the louder she laughed. And her laughter was very infectious. Holly found her lips twitching in spite of herself.

'Do you want me to tell you another one?' Miranda said.

Peter clapped a hand over Miranda's mouth. 'Don't you dare,' he said. 'Holly, don't encourage her.'

But Holly wasn't listening. 'Shh!' she said. 'There's something on the news bulletin I want to hear. Listen!'

'. . . robbery at the stately home ten years ago,' said the newsreader. 'And although Basil Palmer, the thief, was caught, the jewels were never recovered. Palmer always refused to reveal where he had hidden them. The whereabouts of the valuable jewels still baffles police. Their value has been estimated to be over a million pounds.'

'Wow!' said Peter under his breath.

Holly, Peter and Miranda leaned closer to the radio.

'However, the death of Palmer in prison last night means that the mystery will never be solved,' the newsreader went on. 'The secret hiding-place of the family treasure went to the grave with him.'

Miranda looked at the other two, her eyes like saucers.

'The secret went to the grave with him,' she repeated as the newsreader moved on to the weather forecast. 'Now that's what I *call* an unsolved mystery.'

'Imagine that!' said Holly. 'Jewels worth a million pounds – and nobody knows where they are.'

'What stately home was he talking about?' said Peter.

Holly frowned. 'What was it?' she said. 'Oh yes, it sounded like Castle Vilgrand or something.'

'Funny name,' said Miranda.

Holly shrugged. 'Anyway the newsreader said it was somewhere in Hampshire.'

The radio station jingle played and the DJ's voice came on again. 'And now, the moment all you sleuths out there have been waiting for,' he said.

Holly squealed with excitement. 'I'd almost forgotten about the competition,' she said.

'So much for not being able to stand the suspense,' said Peter.

'Shh!' said Miranda. 'This is it.'

'We had a pile of entries,' the DJ was

saying. 'But the only three who got all the answers correct were . . .' He paused and Holly, Peter and Miranda held their breath. 'Holly Adams, Peter Hamilton and Miranda Hunt,' the DJ said.

The Mystery Kids looked at one another, then Miranda leapt to her feet and hugged Holly and Peter.

'We won!' she yelled. 'We won! I can't believe it.'

'Oh, no?' said Holly. 'Who said "of course we'll win"?'

'I didn't really mean that,' said Miranda, her face flushed with pleasure.

The DJ was speaking again. 'And the prize is that wonderful mystery weekend at Granville Towers,' he said. 'So, wait by your phones, Peter, Holly and Miranda. We'll be contacting you to make all the arrangements.'

'A mystery weekend,' said Peter. 'Isn't it great?'

Holly and Miranda nodded, eyes shining.

Miranda screwed up her eyes. 'I've always wanted to go on one,' she said, 'but what exactly *happens* on a mystery weekend?'

Peter shrugged. 'I'm not sure, but we're soon going to find out!'

'Wow! Look at this,' Peter said as his dad's old car swept through the gates and up the driveway to Granville Towers. Mr Hamilton had driven the three of them down to Hampshire.

'It's quite a place,' said Mr Hamilton.

Holly gasped and twisted round to look back the way they had come, her eyes fixed on one of the stone pillars that flanked the gates. 'Did you see the name on that pillar?' she said.

Peter whistled and pointed up ahead.

'No wonder it's called Granville *Towers*,' he said from the front seat beside his dad.

Holly looked. The house seemed to have a hundred towers, all soaring upwards to dizzying heights. There were broad steps in front of the house leading up to a massive front door. Stone lions guarded the entrance.

'It's like a castle,' said Peter.

'It's a bit too Gothic for my taste,' Mr Hamilton said.

'It *is* a castle,' Holly said while Mr Hamilton

brought the car to a halt in front of the steps. 'Didn't you see the name on the pillar at the gates?'

'What – Granville Towers?' said Peter. 'I didn't notice.'

'No,' Holly said. 'Castle Ville Grande.'

'What?' said Miranda, frowning. 'That sounds familiar.'

Holly nodded her head excitedly. 'Of course it does,' she said. 'It's the name of the place that was on the news, the stately home those jewels were stolen from.'

'You mean those jewels that were never found?' Miranda said. 'The secret that went to the grave with what's his name – Palmer?'

Holly nodded. 'It has to be the same place,' she said. 'There can't be *two* places called Castle Ville Grande.'

'So why call it Granville Towers?' said Miranda.

'That's right,' Peter said. 'Why should they change the name?'

Holly looked up at the house as Mr Hamilton got out of the car and strode round to the boot. 'I don't know,' she said. 'But I'd sure like to find out.'

The Granville Treasure

Holly took her bag out of the boot and turned towards the house. A young man with dark hair and a green sweat-shirt came out and stood for a moment on the front steps, looking at them. Holly raised her hand and waved but he didn't wave back.

'He isn't very friendly,' said Miranda as he turned quickly and went back into the house.

'Maybe he didn't see you wave,' said Peter.

But Holly was sure the young man had seen her. 'He was in a bit of a hurry to get back into the house,' she said. 'I wonder why.'

Mr Hamilton smiled. 'Mysteries already,' he teased. 'You three find suspicious happenings wherever you go.'

'And we're usually right,' said Peter.

'Well, they've got a mystery laid on for you this weekend,' Mr Hamilton said. 'So you don't have to find your own!'

'Mmm,' said Miranda. '*And* I've got a whole weekend without Becky and Rachel,' she said. 'That's going to be heaven even without the murder mystery thrown in.'

Becky and Rachel were Miranda's annoying fifteen year old twin sisters.

'And no Jamie either,' said Holly. 'I tell you, one little brother is more trouble than half a dozen sisters!'

'Want to bet?' said Miranda.

Peter lifted the last bag out of the boot. 'I don't know what you two are complaining about,' he said.

Holly and Miranda looked at him. Peter was an only child. His mum had died when he was a baby and it was just him and his dad now.

'Ready?' said Peter's dad.

'Are you coming in, Mr Hamilton?' Holly asked.

He nodded. 'I know they're expecting you,' he said. 'But I want to make sure you get the full star treatment.'

Miranda grinned and swept her hair back. 'I wouldn't mind being a star,' she said as she walked up the front steps, her nose in the air.

'Watch out,' Holly cried as Miranda nearly went head first over one of the big stone lions at the front door.

'Have a good trip?' Peter said.

'Don't *you* start,' Holly said to Peter. 'Miranda's jokes are bad enough.'

The front hall of Granville Towers was magnificent. It had a black and white chequered marble floor and long windows that reached almost to the ceiling. The walls were panelled in dark wood and covered in oil paintings.

'Those must be portraits of all the Granville ancestors,' Holly said looking at the paintings of men and women in old-fashioned clothes.

'Look at the suits of armour,' Miranda hissed, diving behind one and grinning round at them. Then she peered at the shiny metal.

'What are you looking at?' Peter said.

'Not at,' said Miranda. 'I'm looking for bloodstains. You'd think there would be some.'

'Talk about bloodthirsty,' said Peter, but he looked interested. 'Have you found any?'

'No such luck,' said Miranda. 'Somebody has been polishing this. Imagine polishing a suit of armour. You'd think they'd keep the bloodstains. Some people just don't appreciate history.'

'And look at all those antlers on that wall,' said Holly. 'Ugh! I don't know if I like that.'

'And those guns and swords,' said Peter, looking at the weapons arranged on another wall. 'Some of them look hundreds of years old.'

'Cripes,' Miranda said. 'There won't be any shortage of murder weapons, will there?'

'There you are,' a voice said behind them. 'We've been expecting you.'

Holly turned round and stared straight at a smiling, tall fair-haired woman. She was dressed in a blue skirt and jumper.

'I'm Pat Granville,' she said. 'Welcome to Granville Towers.' She looked from one to the other. 'You *are* the Mystery Kids, aren't you?' she said, casting a quick glance at Mr Hamilton.

'How did you know?' said Holly, her eyes wide.

Mrs Granville smiled at Mr Hamilton. 'Oh, we have our methods,' she said.

Peter turned to his father accusingly. 'Dad!' he cried.

Mr Hamilton grinned. 'I told you I wanted to make sure you had the full star treatment, didn't I?' he said. 'Mrs Granville and I had a chat on the phone when I arranged to bring you down.' He looked at his watch. 'I'm off,' he said and smiled at the three of them. 'Enjoy yourselves, you three,' he said. 'And don't get up to any mischief.'

'As if we would!' said Miranda.

'As if you wouldn't!' said Mr Hamilton and shook his head in mock despair.

Pat Granville smiled. 'They won't have time to get up to mischief,' she said. 'They'll be too busy solving clues.'

'Just as well,' said Mr Hamilton as he walked towards the front door. He turned and waved before he went out. 'Happy hunting!' he said.

Mrs Granville turned to the Mystery Kids.

'We're looking forward to you three putting our mystery weekend to the test,' she said.

'Not too big a test,' another voice said and Holly swung round.

A tall man in an ancient jumper and baggy corduroy trousers had come out of a door in the hall. He walked towards them, across the black and white chequered marble floor. He had dark hair and very blue eyes. Holly frowned. He reminded her of someone but she couldn't think who it was.

'We aren't used to having professionals on the job here,' he said.

'This is my husband, James,' said Mrs Granville.

'We were admiring your weapons collection,' Peter said.

'And the suits of armour,' Miranda added. 'They're really shiny.'

Mr Granville smiled. 'I'll tell Mrs Billings you noticed,' he said. 'She's our housekeeper and she's always complaining about dusting them.'

Mrs Granville laughed. 'No wonder,' she said. 'Mrs Billings keeps the whole house spotless almost single-handed. She's a treasure.' She looked round the shining hall.

Miranda turned to Holly. 'Treasure!' she mouthed.

'Shh!' Peter said to her.

But Mrs Granville had heard. 'What was that?' she said.

Peter shuffled uncomfortably. 'It's just that we recognised the house. It was on the news.' He bit his lip. 'At least . . . I mean . . . we think it's the same house.'

'Why has it got two names?' said Miranda. Miranda believed in the direct approach.

Mr Granville ran a hand through his hair. 'Oh, there's no mystery about that,' he said. 'It used to be called Castle Ville Grande,' he paused. 'That's French, you know,' he said. 'The Granvilles came over with the Norman Conquest.'

'Ville Grande . . . Granville,' said Miranda. 'I see.'

'Granville is the family name,' said Mr Granville.

Mrs Granville smiled ruefully. 'When the jewels were stolen, we had a lot of trouble with treasure hunters,' she said.

'Treasure hunters?' Peter queried.

Mr Granville nodded. 'The newspapers started calling the jewels the Granville Treasure,' he said. 'We used to find people creeping round the garden with metal detectors and spades.'

'And of course when we decided to turn the house into a hotel, we couldn't have that kind of thing going on,' said Mrs Granville.

'So we changed the name to Granville Towers,' said Mr Granville. 'I tell you, we've had a lot more peace since then.'

'So, you see, there's no great mystery about the two names,' said Mrs Granville.

'But there is a mystery about the Granville Treasure,' said Miranda.

Mrs Granville sighed. 'And, of course, it was on the news again because of Palmer's death,' she said. She shook her head. 'I hope we don't have a hard time concentrating the guests' minds on the murder mystery this weekend.'

'But is it really true?' said Miranda. 'Were the jewels lost?'

Mr Granville shook his head. 'Nobody knows what happened to them,' he said.

Then he smiled, his eyes twinkling. 'But I give you full permission to look,' he said. 'After all, you're the Mystery Kids.'

Holly grinned. She liked Mr and Mrs Granville and she could see the other two did as well.

'We're really looking forward to the weekend,' she said. 'We've never really *won* anything before.'

James Granville smiled at her. 'Why don't you let Pat show you to your rooms,' he said. 'Then you can explore before dinner.'

'Have you got any secret passages?' Miranda asked.

'Or dungeons?' said Peter.

Mr Granville laughed. 'Not that I've found,' he said. 'But you really are welcome to look for the Granville Treasure if you like.' He looked at his wife and the corners of his mouth turned down. 'Heaven knows, we could do with it,' he said.

Holly looked at Pat Granville and saw her frown slightly.

'Not in front of the guests, dear,' she said. She spread her arms out, herding them towards the staircase. 'Now, come and see your rooms,' she said.

Holly had a good look round as they ascended the staircase. It was amazing. There were two enormous wooden carvings of strange looking creatures at the bottom of it, one on each side.

'What kind of animals are these?' said Miranda. 'They don't look like anything I've ever seen in a zoo.'

Mrs Granville laughed. 'That's because they're mythical animals,' she said. 'One is a dragon and the other's a griffin. They both appear on the Granville coat of arms.'

'Fancy having your own coat of arms,' Miranda said.

The staircase was about three metres wide. It branched at the top into a wide gallery that swept in a semi-circle round the hall. Holly looked down as they walked along the gallery towards one of the corridors that ran off it.

'Wow! look at the hall from up here,' she said. She could see past the chandeliers that hung from the roof far above.

Peter hung over the banister and gazed down. 'From up here those suits of armour look like chessmen on that chequered floor,' he said.

Miranda leaned on the banister beside him. 'They'd be a bit heavy to move around,' she said. Then she grinned. 'We could get inside and pretend to be chessmen,' she said.

Mrs Granville laughed. 'Don't you dare,' she said. 'You'd frighten the living daylights out of the other guests.'

'Oh, who are they?' said Miranda.

Mrs Granville counted off on her fingers. 'There's a Miss Finch, who's a retired school teacher. Then there's Mr and Mrs Partridge. Mr Partridge used to be a butcher but he's retired now too.'

'A butcher,' said Miranda. 'Just think of all those knives and cleavers and things – perfect murder weapons!'

'Then there are the Martins,' Mrs Granville went on. 'I think Mr Martin is in computers. And Mr Thomson. I gather he wants to do some research.'

'Research?' said Peter. 'What kind?'

Mrs Granville shrugged. 'I don't know,' she said. 'I only spoke to him briefly on the phone. None of the others have arrived yet but they should be here in time for dinner. The dining-room is the room on the right of the front door. It has a wonderful view of the lawns.'

'You must be so proud of this house,' Holly said to Mrs Granville.

Mrs Granville smiled but there was a worried little frown between her brows.

'So long as we can keep it,' she said.

'What do you mean?' said Peter. 'You wouldn't sell it, would you?'

Mrs Granville shrugged. 'We might have to,' she said. 'Houses like this used to have lots of servants but now there's only James and myself and Mrs Billings. Of course, our sons help when they're at home but they are both at university. A house like this costs a fortune to maintain and we haven't got a fortune.' She smiled ruefully. 'Not any more.'

Holly sighed. She supposed lots of old families didn't have the money to keep up houses like this any more. It was a pity all the same.

'At least turning it into a hotel lets everybody enjoy it,' Holly said.

Mrs Granville smiled again. 'Exactly,' she

said. 'That's just what I think. And I hope we can continue to do that.'

She led them into a corridor on the far side of the gallery and opened two doors on the left. 'Now, here are your rooms,' she said. 'I've put you two girls in together. I hope that's OK.'

'Perfect,' said Holly as she walked past Mrs Granville into the room. It was enormous. She opened a door and peered in. 'We've even got our own bathroom!' she said.

'Wow!' said Miranda, coming in after her with Peter. 'You could fit our whole house into this room. And look!'

Holly followed Miranda's gaze. There was a huge basket of dried flowers on a table under the middle of the three enormous windows. The windows looked out over the lawns in front of the house. A few birds strutted across the grass, dragging long tails behind them.

'Peacocks,' said Peter.

There were flowerbeds and, further off, a large area covered in what looked like overgrown bushes.

'I grow most of my flowers round the back of the house in the walled garden and greenhouse,' Mrs Granville said. She looked at the basket of dried flowers. 'I dry them and also use them to make oils.'

'Oils?' said Peter.

'You mean for potpourris and bath oils and stuff?' Miranda said.

Mrs Granville nodded. 'Yes,' she said. 'I leave samples in all the bathrooms.'

Miranda disappeared into the bathroom. 'Lavender, geranium and marjoram,' she said as she came back into the room. She held up a small brown bottle of bath oil. 'It says on the label that this one is for relaxing.'

Mrs Granville nodded. 'I'll need to make some more of that one,' she said. 'It's very popular. In fact I've used the last of that lot for the bedrooms this weekend.' She turned to Peter. 'Peter, your room is just next door. I must start preparing dinner but the three of you are free to go anywhere in the house until then. You'll hear the dinner gong five minutes before we're ready to serve.'

Miranda looked suspicious. 'We don't have to get all dressed up, do we?' she said.

Mrs Granville laughed. 'Some of the older guests like to,' she said. 'But you don't have to bother.'

Miranda looked relieved.

'When does the mystery start?' Peter asked.

Mrs Granville's eyes twinkled. 'How do you know it hasn't started already?' she said with a smile. 'James will tell you all about it at dinner.'

'We saw somebody as we arrived,' Holly said. 'He looked about twenty – dark hair, tall.'

'Oh, that would be Mark,' Mrs Granville said.

'Mark?' said Miranda. 'Is he a guest too?'

Mrs Granville smiled. 'He's here for the mystery weekend as well,' she said. 'He drove down earlier. Oh, I nearly forgot. You'll find a sheet of paper with the background story on your bedside table.'

Miranda whirled round and pounced on the bedside table. 'Oooh!' she said, rolling her eyes dramatically as she waved the sheet of paper at them. 'Sir Reginald has been murdered!'

Mrs Granville laughed. 'I'll leave you to

get on with it,' she said. 'You'll get the rest of your instructions after dinner.'

'It sounds mysterious already,' said Holly.

'Good,' said Mrs Granville. 'It's supposed to.' She turned to go out of the room, then stopped. 'Just one thing,' she said. 'If you go out on the battlements, don't lean over too far. We don't want a *real* body, do we?'

'Battlements!' squeaked Miranda.

Mrs Granville grinned. 'Top landing and out through any of the long windows,' she said. 'I've never met anyone who could resist them. Our boys used to play on the roof more than they played in the garden!'

'Cripes!' said Peter after Mrs Granville had gone. 'What a place. Can you believe it? I'll just dump my stuff, then we'll explore.'

'So what exactly happened to Sir Reginald?' Holly said as Peter left the room.

Miranda began to read. 'Poisoned,' she said. 'Cyanide in his cocoa.' She looked up. 'He had a mug of cocoa every night before going to bed.'

Holly came and stood beside her. 'All his family were here at the time,' she said, reading over Miranda's shoulder. 'Oh, and the guests are supposed to be his family.' She grinned. 'You, Peter and I are his grandchildren according to this.'

'Oh, dear old grandfather,' Miranda said tragically. She collapsed on to the nearest bed and buried her head in her arms.

'You don't actually have to do the acting bit,' said Holly. 'All this stuff is just background to put you in the picture.'

'Oh, all right,' said Miranda. 'If you don't like my acting, I can take a hint.' She sat up and smoothed out the crumpled instructions. 'Miss Finch, Mr Martin and Mr Thomson are supposed to be Sir Reginald's children and Mark is another grandchild.' She looked up at Holly. 'And they all need money,' she said. 'Including us!'

Holly sat down beside Miranda. 'One of them saw the murderer,' she read.

'And now the murderer is after the witness,' Miranda said.

They looked at each other. 'That must be what we're here to solve,' said Miranda.

'Only the second murder hasn't happened yet,' said Holly.

Peter came into their room. 'What hasn't happened yet?' he said.

'The murder,' Miranda said. 'I wonder how it's going to be done.'

'There are all those swords and guns hanging on the walls,' said Holly. 'That's one way to bump off somebody.'

'And the battlements,' said Peter. 'Shoving somebody over the battlements could be the perfect way of murdering them. Let's go and check it out.'

The girls followed him out of the room and Holly looked over the banister. 'You wouldn't need to bother with the battlements,' she said. 'Look down there.'

The three of them craned over the banister and gazed down on the black and white marble floor below.

'It makes you dizzy looking at all those checks from up here,' Peter said.

'Wow!' Miranda said. 'I'm impressed. I've never been in a house before that had so many ways of murdering somebody.'

Peter grinned as they started to climb the stairs to the top floor. 'I wonder how the murderer is going to do it,' he pondered.

'I wonder when it'll be,' Miranda added.

'Not until after dinner anyway,' said Holly.

Peter shook his head. 'That could be a red herring. You know, something to mislead us,' he said. 'Maybe the murder mystery *has* started already, like Mrs Granville said.'

The Mystery Kids looked at one another in silence.

'Does Mr Granville remind you of anyone?' Holly said suddenly.

'No,' said Miranda. 'What do you mean?'

Peter shook his head. 'Me neither,' he said. 'What makes you say that?'

Holly looked puzzled. 'I don't know,' she said. 'I just have this feeling that maybe I've seen him before – or someone awfully like him.'

'Imagination!' said Miranda. 'You'll be hearing things next!'

Suddenly a scream rang out and they froze.

'What was that?' said Holly at last.

Peter and Miranda looked at each other.

'I don't know,' said Peter, 'but we can't all be hearing things. I guess we'd better find out!'

Who screamed?

'Where did it come from?' said Peter.

Holly looked towards the top landing. 'Up there,' she said and she started to run up the stairs.

'Quick!' Miranda said. 'That scream sounded terrible. Somebody must be in trouble.'

Holly's feet pounded up the stairs as she raced towards the top landing with its floor-to-ceiling windows. She got to the top first. She looked round the empty landing and ran a hand through her hair.

'There's nobody here,' she said, puzzled.

'But there must be,' said Miranda. 'The scream came from up here.' She frowned. 'We didn't imagine it, did we?'

'We couldn't all have imagined it,' said Peter.

'But nobody passed us on the stairs,' said Miranda.

Peter shrugged. 'Then whoever it was has disappeared,' he said. 'There's no one here now.'

'Except the Honourable Amelia Granville,' Miranda said, standing in front of an enormous portrait of a woman in a crinoline dress. 'And she doesn't look too happy.'

Holly looked at the Honourable Amelia and then down at her own T-shirt and jeans. 'No wonder,' she said. 'Imagine having to wear stuff like that.'

'Look at that necklace,' Miranda said.

'It must have been worth a fortune, Holly breathed.'

'Maybe it's part of the Granville Treasure,' Miranda said.

Just then there was another terrifying scream. The Mystery Kids looked at one another.

'It came from outside,' said Peter, running towards one of the floor-to-ceiling windows.

'From the roof?' said Miranda.

Holly's heart leapt. It was all very well to joke about somebody being shoved over the battlements but what if it had actually happened?

Peter slid one of the long windows up and scrambled over the sill on to the roof. Holly and Miranda were right behind him as he raced towards the battlements.

'Be careful, Peter,' Holly yelled as she saw him reach them and lean over.

'What is it?' shouted Miranda as she and Holly raced for the battlements. 'Has somebody fallen off the roof?'

Peter turned to face them. 'It's a peacock!' he said, pointing.

Holly and Miranda leaned over and looked where he was pointing.

'It's roosting on that turret down there,' said Miranda, spluttering with laughter.

Peter shook his head. 'I know peacocks roost in trees,' he said. 'But I've never seen one roosting on a roof before!'

'And, of course, peacocks scream,' said Holly. She looked down at the bird perched on the turret, its long tail dangling. Far below them more peacocks were strutting across the lawn. One had its tail spread out in all its glory.

'You can see for miles from up here,' Holly said. 'Right across the lawns and out over farms and there's a river in the distance.'

'It must have been great in the olden days,' Peter said. 'You'd see the enemy coming from far away. You'd have loads of time to get the boiling oil and the arrows and the cannon ready.'

'You could throw boulders down,' said Miranda, getting into the spirit of the thing.

'Look, there are some people down there,' Holly said. 'They look tiny!'

'They must be the other guests,' said Peter. 'I wonder which one's the murderer.'

'Imagine they're the enemy,' Miranda said. 'And we're up here with the boiling oil and the arrows.' She turned to Holly but Holly was squinting at the hedges in the garden.

'What are you looking at?' she said.

Holly frowned. 'It's those hedges,' she said. 'I'm sure I can see a pattern of some sort.' She put her hand up to shade her eyes and squeezed them up even more tightly.

'That's better,' she said, then her breath caught in an excited gasp. 'Oh, I know what it is,' she said.

'What what is?' said Peter.

Holly pointed to the mass of hedge. 'That,' she said. 'See if you can see it too.'

Peter and Miranda half-closed their eyes. Miranda's tongue was poking out in concentration.

'I can't see anything,' she said.

'What are we supposed to be looking for?' said Peter.

'Look closely,' said Holly. 'You can see where the hedge is different colours. Some bits of it are much lighter than others. You must see it. It's as if there are lines of lighter-coloured hedge running through. And in some places there are gaps.'

'I see that,' said Peter.

'So?' said Miranda.

Holly turned to her. 'So it's a maze,' she said. 'Only it's so overgrown that it's really hard to see the design of it. The hedge must have grown up and hidden the paths.'

'You mean there are paths in amongst that?' said Peter.

'Like a maze tunnel,' said Miranda.

Holly nodded. 'That's what it looks like to me. I'm sure I can see something right in the middle of it.'

'What? Where?' said Miranda, peering into the distance.

Holly pointed. 'There,' she said. 'There's an open area in the middle. You can just see the edge of something. It looks like a statue.'

'I can't make it out,' Miranda said. 'But we can check with Mrs Granville.' She grinned. 'This place really has got everything!' she said.

'Let's go and have a closer look at it,' Peter said.

'Race you down,' Miranda called and was off, scrambling over the windowsill and racing downstairs.

Holly and Peter chased after her, past the portraits of long dead Granvilles and down into the entrance hall. Suddenly Miranda halted and Peter and Holly cannoned into her.

'No wonder you thought you'd seen Mr Granville somewhere before,' she said.

'What?' said Holly.

Miranda swept her hand in a wide arc round the walls of the staircase and hall. 'Look!' she said. 'The place is full of them.'

'Of course,' said Peter. 'Mr Granville's

ancestors. Look at that one of the guy in the feathered hat. That could be Mr Granville's twin brother. You must have recognised his face from all these portraits, Holly.'

Holly looked at the pictures. A surprising number of the people in them had dark hair and very blue eyes.

'That must be it,' she said. The portraits had been one of the first things she had noticed when they had arrived at the house.

'And here come the other guests!' said Peter as they heard the sound of voices.

There was a group of people just coming in through the front door.

'Come on!' Miranda said, dragging Holly and Peter behind a suit of armour.

'What are you hiding for?' Holly said.

Miranda peered round the screen. 'I want to get a good look at them before they see us,' she said. 'You know, to suss out the competition.'

Holly stuck her head round the suit of armour too.

There was a plump lady with a mop of bright red hair and a voice nearly as loud as Miranda's. She seemed to be with a small man who kept pulling at his tie, as if it was too tight for him.

'I'll bet they're the Partridges,' Peter said.

Holly and Miranda nodded.

'And that's got to be the Martins,' Holly said, pointing to a youngish couple. The man had a short fair beard and the woman had mousey-coloured hair. She looked a bit apprehensive.

Next there was a thin man with dark hair and a very pale face.

'Mr Thomson, the researcher,' Peter said firmly.

'So that must be Miss Finch,' said Miranda, looking at an elderly lady with half-moon glasses and grey hair done up in an untidy bun. She seemed to be wearing rather a lot of filmy scarves round her neck and shoulders.

'Why have they all arrived together?' Peter said. 'That's suspicious.'

Mrs Granville came out of a doorway and into the hall.

'Hello, James,' she said as Mr Granville came through the front door and she smiled at the guests. 'I see my husband was in time to meet the train,' she said.

'Mystery solved,' said Holly.

As Mrs Granville led the guests off upstairs, the young man they had seen earlier came in through the front door. Mrs Granville had said his name was Mark. Mr Granville said something to him and the two of them walked towards a green baize door at the end of the hall. They disappeared through the door.

'I wonder where that door leads,' said Miranda.

'Come on,' Peter said. 'Let's go.'

Holly hesitated.

'Holly,' said Miranda. 'We've got a maze to explore. What are you waiting for?' And she hurtled out of the front door after Peter.

Holly looked at the green baize door at the end of the hall. There was something about Mark . . . Well, maybe it would come to her later.

'Wait for me!' she yelled as she raced across the chequered floor to the open front door.

The Mystery Kids ran down the lawns towards the maze. 'Oh, no, a gate,' Miranda wailed as they approached maze. 'I bet it's locked!'

Holly was the first to reach the maze. She tugged at the gate. It was made of iron and quite high. And it *was* locked.

'We could climb in,' Peter said.

But Holly shook her head. 'If it's locked, there must be a reason. We can't go exploring in places that are obviously out of bounds. What if Mrs Granville sent us home before the mystery weekend had even begun?'

Peter nodded. 'I suppose you're right,' he said. 'Why don't we go and ask permission?'

'We can ask for the key,' Miranda said. 'There must be one.'

Peter looked at the gate again. 'That gate is so rusty a key probably wouldn't be any good,' he said. 'It looks as if it hasn't been opened in years. Look at all the leaf mould that's gathered in there.' He stuck his foot under the gate. 'I wonder *why* it's all locked up,' he said.

Holly looked at the rusty lock. Peter was right. It clearly hadn't been used for a long time.

'We can ask if we can climb in even if we can't unlock the gate,' she said.

'I've always wanted to solve a maze,'

Miranda said. 'Do you think Mrs Granville will let us try?'

Peter shook his head. 'Who knows?' he said. 'She was pretty good about us going up on to the roof. She might.'

'I'm going to ask her right now,' Miranda said.

She turned back towards the house just as a deep booming sound echoed across the garden from the front door.

'What's that?' said Peter.

Holly listened. The sound came again.

'I guess that's the dinner gong,' she said. 'Race you to the house!'

Miranda was first through the front door. The Mystery Kids came to an abrupt halt just as a small plump woman came through the green baize door at the end of the hall. She was carrying a tray of food. So the door obviously led to the kitchens.

Now why had Mark gone to the kitchens with Mr Granville? Holly wondered.

'Well, well,' the small plump woman said. 'Now I hope you three have got good appetites.'

Holly grinned. 'You must be Mrs Billings,' she said.

Mrs Billings nodded. Then she looked at them more closely. 'And where have you been?' she said. 'Up the chimneys?'

Miranda giggled, then she looked at her hands. 'Good guess!' she said. 'We were up on the roof. It was pretty mucky up there.'

'I'm starving,' Peter said.

The girls laughed. 'You're always starving,' Holly said.

'Show me a boy who isn't,' said Mrs Billings. 'But you can't go into my dining-room in that state.' She nodded towards a door under the stairs. 'You can wash your hands in the downstairs cloakroom,' she said. 'I'll save you a crust or two.'

'And I've always wanted to come on a mystery weekend so when my Joe said to me "Edna, let's treat ourselves," this was what we decided to do.' Mrs Partridge finished on a breathless note and Holly gave Miranda a wink.

'Poor little Mr Partridge doesn't get a word in edgeways,' Miranda whispered in her ear.

Holly looked round the big dining table. The dining-room was as magnificent as the rest of the house, with more portraits on the walls and a log fire burning in the massive fireplace. The table was huge too – it certainly could have accommodated more than the twelve people who sat round it. There were Mr and Mrs Partridge, Mark, the Martins, Miss Finch and the pale man whose name was Thomson. Mr and Mrs Granville sat at either end of the long table and kept the conversation going. Not that there was much difficulty there. Everybody loved mystery stories and soon they were swapping names of their favourite authors and books.

'Agatha Christie is our favourite,' Mr Partridge confided to Holly while his wife was helping herself to more vegetables.

'Our favourite book is *Harriet the Spy*,' said Miranda. 'It's brilliant.'

'PJ Benson,' said Mark suddenly. 'That's my all-time favourite.'

Holly frowned. 'I've never heard of PJ Benson,' she said.

'Really?' said Mark. 'You must have.'

Holly shook her head and looked at the other two. Peter shrugged his shoulders and Miranda raised her eyebrows.

'I'll lend you some after dinner,' he said. 'I've got a stack of them in the . . .'

Mrs Granville coughed and Mark looked towards her.

'I mean I think I've brought one with me,' he said.

Holly narrowed her eyes. Mark's face had flushed very slightly.

Mrs Partridge asked Mr Thomson who his favourite detective novelist was.

Mr Thomson looked up. 'What did you say?' he said.

'I said who is your favourite detective novelist,' Mrs Partridge said slowly as if Mr Thomson were hard of hearing.

Mr Thomson shook his head. 'I haven't got one really,' he said.

'But you must have or you wouldn't be here on a mystery weekend,' Mrs Partridge said.

Mr Thomson looked embarrassed. 'Actually, I'm writing a detective story,' he said. 'That's why I'm here.' He smiled nervously and cleared his throat. 'You could call it research, I suppose,' he said.

'Writing a book?' Miranda squealed, her eyes round as saucers. 'A detective novel? Oh, that's wonderful. What's it about?'

Mr Thomson looked at her warily. 'I haven't quite decided yet,' he mumbled.

Mrs Partridge began telling them all the plot of the last Agatha Christie she had read. Then Mrs Granville announced coffee in the lounge.

'And with your coffee – your instructions,' Mr Granville said, rising from the table.

'I want to talk to Mr Thomson,' Miranda said to Holly.

'Why?' said Holly.

Miranda looked at her in disbelief. 'He's writing a detective novel,' she said. 'I want to know where he gets all his ideas from.'

Holly narrowly avoided getting stuck beside Mrs Partridge and sat down beside Miss Finch. She could see Peter talking to Mrs Granville. Mrs Granville was shaking her head and Peter looked disappointed. Holly thought she could guess what they were talking about. The maze.

Miss Finch had taught in North London before she retired and knew one or two of Holly's teachers.

'I'd better be on my best behaviour then,' Holly said, picking up one of Miss Finch's scarves that had slid to the floor.

Miss Finch's eyes twinkled. 'Oh, you don't have to worry about me reporting back,' she said. Then she looked up. 'I see Mrs Granville is free, I must just go and ask her about those wonderful dried flower arrangements.'

Holly watched as Miss Finch drifted across the room, casting scarves as she went.

Peter had finished talking to Mrs Granville. He came over to sit beside Holly.

'No luck with the maze then?' she said.

Peter grinned. 'How did you know I was talking to Mrs Granville about that?' he said.

Holly tapped the side of her nose. 'Just my amazing powers of deduction.'

Miranda came across the room and flopped on a footstool in front of them. 'Well, that was a dead loss,' she said.

'Mr Thomson?' Holly said.

Miranda nodded. 'This is his first detective novel. In fact it's his first book,' she said. 'And

I'm sure I know more about detective stories and mystery books than he does. I don't think he's ever *read* a mystery book. He has no idea what his book's even going to be about.'

Holly looked thoughtful. 'That's odd,' she said. 'But I suppose everybody has to start somewhere, even mystery writers. Maybe when he's written his book he'll give us an interview for the magazine.'

'Or a copy of the book to review,' said Miranda, brightening up. 'He might even have a plot worked out by the end of the weekend. I'll ask him.' She looked at Peter. 'Did you ask about the maze?'

Peter shook his head. 'No go,' he said. 'Mrs Granville says we aren't to go near it. She says the key disappeared years ago. She reckons if we went in we might never get out.'

'Disappeared?' Holly repeated. 'Another mystery!'

Miranda shivered. 'Imagine wandering round the maze till you died of starvation and in years to come all they'd find would be a little pile of bones,' she said.

Holly gave her a shove. 'I reckon if you got stuck in that maze you'd yell so hard the whole of Hampshire would hear you,' she teased.

'Can I have your attention?' Mr Granville called.

At once the hum of chatter stopped and everybody looked at Mr Granville.

He smiled round at them and held up a sheaf of envelopes and some papers.

'I am your Mystery Master for the weekend and in my hand I have an envelope and a plan of the house for each of you,' he said. 'Inside the envelope you will find your instructions.' He dropped his voice slightly. 'One of you is the murderer and it is up to the rest to find out who that person is. I trust you have all read the outline story in your room?'

Everybody nodded.

'Sir Reginald has been murdered,' Mr Granville said. He looked round all the guests. 'You are Sir Reginald's family and you all had a reason for murdering him – money! One of you did it and one of you saw who did it. The murderer knows that he or she was seen and is going to murder again.

'Who is the next victim and who is the murderer? Each envelope contains a white card. Eight of these cards are blank. One card has a red cross on it. If you find that card in your envelope then you are the victim.' A murmur ran round the room and Miranda wriggled with excitement.

Mr Granville went on. 'Another card has a black cross on it. If you find that card in your envelope then you are the murderer.' Mr Granville paused.

'Oooh,' said Mrs Partridge, shivering. 'It feels real, doesn't it?'

Mr Granville handed out the envelopes and the plans. Miranda made to open her envelope.

'One moment,' Mr Granville said.

They all looked up.

'You will see your name and a room on the front of the envelope. I want you to go to the room assigned to you, open your envelope and then dispose of the information in it. That way nobody can possibly know who has the murderer's envelope.' His eyes twinkled. 'Of course I shall know where the murderer and the victim will be – and I shall find you and give you the rest of your instructions.'

Holly, Peter and Miranda looked at one another.

'That's pretty smart,' said Peter, then he grinned. 'Hey, we'll be suspecting one another.'

Miranda narrowed her eyes. 'Watch out then,' she said. 'I've been studying Sherlock Holmes! Nothing gets by me!'

Holly looked at her envelope. 'The billiards room,' she said.

'I've got the dining-room,' Peter said.

'And I'm in the downstairs cloakroom,' Miranda said. 'OK, let's go!'

One by one the guests drifted out of the room, the envelopes clutched in their hands.

Holly saw Mrs Partridge make for the stairs and Miss Finch disappear through a doorway in the hall which she thought led to the garden room.

'Back to the lounge in fifteen minutes,' Mr Granville said.

Holly made her way to the billiards room and opened her envelope. She sighed with relief. There was no red cross denoting the murderer and no black one denoting the victim. She was glad. She would much rather be a detective. But now she had to get rid of the evidence.

She looked towards the fireplace but there was no fire. She tore the blank sheet of paper into the tiniest pieces and dropped them in the grate, then she made her way back to the lounge. She was halfway along the corridor when there was an almighty crash and the sound of breaking glass. Suddenly the hall was full of people as guests came running from all over the house.

'Where did it come from?' shouted Mrs Partridge.

'The library, I think,' Mark said.

Miranda looked at her plan of the house. 'This way,' she said.

They made a dash for the library, falling over one another in their haste to get there. They stopped in the doorway. The big library windows were divided into small panes. There was a jagged break in one of these. Lying on the floor was a brick with a piece of paper wrapped round it.

Miss Finch made a dive for it.

'Should we touch it?' Mrs Martin cried, clutching her husband's arm.

'What else do you suggest?' Mrs Partridge said. She marched over and picked up the brick.

Swiftly she unwrapped the paper.

'What does it say?' Peter asked.

Mrs Partridge looked at them all. She cleared her throat. 'It says "I shall kill. Will it be tonight? Be on your guard!"'

Miranda gave a little scream and Holly gasped. The mystery had begun!

An inside-out clue

There was a sound at the door and Mr Granville came into the room. He looked around, then he smiled. 'Well,' he said. 'This is it! Get sleuthing.'

Miranda whipped her notebook out of her jeans pocket, looked at her watch, wrote down the time and began to scribble furiously.

'Clues,' said Holly. 'We've got to look for clues.' She looked at the other guests; then a thought occurred to her. Was the murderer here in the room? She cast a glance round the room and counted. They were all there, all ten of them. Nobody was missing.

Holly tried to remember who had come from where but there had been such confusion when the crash sounded and everybody rushed into the hall that she couldn't be sure of anything. Whoever had thrown that brick must have been outside but who was it? They had all been in different parts of the house at the time.

Mr Granville smiled at her. 'I see you've realised the difficulty,' he said. 'Any one of you could have thrown that brick. Any one of you could be the murderer. And whoever is the murderer will be trying to throw the others off the scent.'

'You mean we can't trust one another?' Peter said, looking at Holly and Miranda.

Mr Granville nodded. 'The murderer will tell lies,' he said. 'None of you can afford to trust anybody else – not until you've eliminated that person as a suspect.'

Miranda looked from Peter to Holly. 'But we *always* work together,' she wailed.

Peter sighed. 'Not this time, Miranda,' he said. 'Anyway, where were you when the brick came through the window?'

'In the downstairs cloakroom,' Miranda said.

'You're lying,' said Peter.

'Peter!' Miranda squealed, outraged.

'Well, you could be if you were the murderer,' he said.

'But I'm not lying,' said Miranda. Then her eyes grew round. 'Oh, I see what you mean,' she said. 'I'd say that anyway, wouldn't I, even if I *were* the murderer?'

'*Especially* if you were the murderer,' Peter said.

Mrs Martin looked at her husband. 'Does that mean I have to suspect you, Jeremy?' she said.

Mr Martin patted her hand. 'Of course not, dear,' he said.

Mrs Partridge sniffed. 'Hmph,' she said, tossing her head and making her mop of red hair dance. 'I wouldn't trust a word he says, Mrs Martin,' she pronounced. And she looked Mr Martin straight in the eye.

Mr Martin fingered his beard nervously and coughed.

Mrs Martin gave her husband a look. 'Mr Granville,' she said, 'can I just check the layout of the house with you?' And she and Mr Granville disappeared through the library door.

Holly shook her head. 'It's weird having to be suspicious of one another,' she said.

Peter grinned. 'Well, it's only for the

weekend,' he said. 'Come on. If we don't get going the others will have found all the clues before we've even started looking.' He narrowed his eyes. 'But remember, no sharing of clues. One of us could be the murderer.'

Holly sighed and took out her own notebook.

For the next few minutes, everybody was questioning one another. Then Holly went to the window and studied it carefully. There was something not quite right but she couldn't think what it was. Then light dawned as she looked at the floor in front of the broken window. Talk about an inside-out clue! It was just like the book Peter had loaned her. She began to scribble in her notebook.

'I'm going outside,' Mrs Partridge was saying. 'I'm sure there will be footprints in the flowerbeds. There always are in Agatha Christie books.'

'That's right,' said Miss Finch, pushing her spectacles up her nose. 'But before we go, can I see everyone's shoes please? If anybody has been in the flowerbeds there will be mud on their shoes.'

Obediently, everyone lifted their feet for Miss Finch to inspect. But nobody had any mud on their shoes except Peter.

'It's leaf mould,' he protested to Miss Finch as she peered accusingly at him through her spectacles.

'It is leaf mould,' said Miranda. 'We were down looking at the maze this afternoon.'

Mr Thomson turned to Peter. 'The maze?' he said.

Peter nodded. 'You can hardly tell it's a maze it's so overgrown, but that's where my trainers got dirty.'

'A likely story,' Mr Martin said, fingering his beard again. 'I think this looks suspicious.'

Everyone wrote something down in their notebooks and Peter looked miserable. Then he brightened up. 'It's quite interesting to be suspected,' he said to Holly.

Miranda stuck her nose in the air. 'Don't think you can play the innocent with me, Peter Hamilton,' she said.

Peter looked at Holly. 'You don't think I'm the murderer, do you?' he said.

Holly smiled secretly. 'Not on the evidence of your trainers,' she said.

'Aha!' Peter said. 'You've found a clue.'

Holly just smiled again. Then she looked at Miranda. 'What's that?' she said.

Miranda stuffed a scrap of paper into her jeans pocket. 'Nothing,' she said.

'It's a clue,' said Peter. 'Go on, show it to us.'

Miranda shook her head. 'You're high on the suspect list already, Peter,' she said. 'And even if you aren't the murderer, Holly might be.'

The three of them looked at one another. It was sinking in that for once the Mystery Kids weren't going to be a team. And it just didn't seem right.

Holly, Peter and Miranda trooped out of the library. Peter wanted to go outside and look for clues and Miranda wanted to find Mr Granville but Holly decided to stay. What she wanted to do was watch the library, to see if anyone came back. After all, Miranda had picked something up off the floor. Whoever had dropped it might come back for it.

'You two go ahead,' said Holly.

Peter and Miranda looked at her suspiciously but didn't say anything. Holly watched them go. Then she scampered along the hall and hid herself behind one of the suits of armour. From there she had a really good view into the library.

Three people came back to the library. First Mr Thomson had a look around and came out again. Then Mark, who took a book from one of the library shelves and left. But it was the third arrival that interested Holly most. The person scrutinised the floor in front of the window and spent several minutes looking round the library, searching for something. Holly wrote all three names down in her notebook. She looked at the third name and shook her head. Now why had Peter sneaked back to the library?

'Holly, pay attention!' said Miranda.

'What?' said Holly. The Mystery Kids had gathered in the billiards room to write up their notes properly. But Holly hadn't been thinking about the murder mystery. She had been thinking about the Granville Treasure. How could all those jewels just disappear into thin air?

'Look!' Miranda said. 'Granville Towers

seems to be just stuffed with mysteries. But we don't stand a chance of solving any of them unless we're in it together.'

'And *that's* the problem,' said Peter.

'OK, you three?' said a voice from the doorway. It was Mr Granville. He came into the room and the door swung to behind him.

'Fine thanks,' said Peter.

Holly bit her lip. 'Mr Granville,' she said. 'Can I ask you something?'

Mr Granville's eyes twinkled. 'So long as it isn't "who is the murderer?"' he said. 'Fire away.'

Holly hesitated, unsure how to start. 'It isn't about the murder mystery. It's about the Granville Treasure,' she said. 'I mean, I suppose there was a really thorough search after the robbery.'

Mr Granville's face took on a weary look. 'Search!' he said. 'The police almost took the place to bits – and so did we,' he added. 'I'm afraid that not a single jewel was ever found and never will be now that Palmer is dead.'

'But what could have happened to them?' Holly said.

Mr Granville shook his head. 'Lord knows,'

he said. 'There were no jewels on him when the police caught Palmer. He was arrested trying to hitch a lift on the London road. We disturbed him, you see, and he made a run for it.'

'But they couldn't just disappear,' said Miranda.

Mr Granville spread his hands. 'We looked in places you wouldn't believe,' he said. 'But there was an hour or so between us disturbing Palmer and him being arrested. He had plenty of time to hide the stuff.'

'But why wouldn't he say where?' said Miranda.

Mr Granville pursed his lips. 'He was stubborn,' he said. 'I reckon he thought he'd serve a few years in prison and then come out and get the stuff from wherever he'd hidden it. I tell you, it made it awkward for us – quite apart from losing the jewels.'

'Why?' said Peter.

Mr Granville gave a rueful smile. 'There were some people who thought we were in it with Palmer.'

'What?' said Holly and Miranda together.

'Oh, yes,' said Mr Granville. 'There were

rumours that we'd made a deal with him to steal the stuff, collect the insurance and then get the jewels back as well.'

'But that's terrible,' said Miranda. 'How could people think a thing like that?'

'All too easily,' said Mr Granville. 'Still, not so many think it now. I mean we wouldn't have had to turn our home into a hotel if we had the family jewels to sell would we?'

'You mean some people *still* think it?' said Holly.

Mr Granville's mouth set in a grim line. 'Some do, I'm afraid,' he said. 'Oh, I don't mind so much for myself but Pat takes it hard if anybody hints at it.' He smiled. 'Mrs Billings is our only Granville treasure now.' He was trying to make a joke of it but his eyes looked worried.

Miranda sighed. 'The Granville Treasure. It must have been wonderful,' she said.

Mr Granville laughed. 'If you're interested in seeing what it was like, just take a look at the portraits in the hall,' he said. 'The Granville ladies were all painted wearing the family jewels.'

'Like the Honourable Amelia,' said Miranda.

Mr Granville grinned. 'The earlier portraits aren't too bad but in the later ones you feel quite sorry for the poor women, they're so weighed down with necklaces and rings and stuff. Most of it's rather ugly.' He scratched his head. 'Still, ugly or not,' he said, 'a necklace or two would pay for a new roof for this place. I don't know how long we can keep going here.'

'But it's your home,' Holly protested.

Mr Granville looked at her. 'Good heavens,' he said. 'I don't know what got into me, talking to you three like this.' He smiled. 'You're good listeners, that's what it is,' he said.

The Mystery Kids grinned at him.

'We're just nosy,' said Miranda.

Mr Granville threw back his head and laughed. 'All good investigators are nosy,' he said. 'Come along and join the others.'

As Miranda passed him, something fell out of her notebook and Mr Granville bent and picked it up.

'Have you been doing geometry homework?' he said.

Miranda looked at him curiously. 'It's a clue,' she said. 'I found it in the library.'

Mr Granville shook his head and handed the paper back to Miranda. 'It isn't a clue for our murder mystery,' he said. 'Or one of my red herrings. Somebody must have dropped it.'

Miranda frowned. 'So it wasn't meant to be there?'

Mr Granville shook his head. 'I've never seen it before,' he said. 'You've come up with more clues than I laid,' he laughed. 'Now that's what I call detecting.'

There was a sound outside the door and Mr Granville swung round. 'Who's there?' he called. There was no answer.

'A spy,' said Holly and made for the door.

She was just in time to see a dark figure disappearing round the corner into the Great Hall. Holly started to run. She had just got to the corner when there was the most almighty crash and a suit of armour fell in her path with a terrible clatter. Holly jumped, narrowly missing falling over it. By the time she had recovered the hall was empty.

'What on earth happened?' Mr Granville said coming out of the billiards room.

Holly looked at Peter and Miranda standing behind him. 'It *was* a spy,' she said. 'But whoever it was got away. They must have been trying to hear what we'd found out.'

'Which is precisely nothing,' said Peter.

Miranda nodded. 'And it's likely to stay that way with the three of us working separately,' she said.

'But why *can't* we pool our resources?' Peter said.

'Because we're all suspects,' said Miranda, 'or had you forgotten?'

Peter shook his head. 'I know that,' he said. 'I mean, why don't we try to eliminate one another? Then we can work on the mystery together?'

'Oh, I see,' said Miranda. She nodded slowly. 'That's brilliant!' she said. 'How unlike you, Peter!'

'Are you going to stick up for me?' Peter said, turning to Holly. Then he stopped. 'What's the matter?' he said.

Holly folded her arms and looked Peter straight in the eye. 'I'm not pooling any resources until I've got an answer to a question,' she said.

'Like who knocked that suit of armour over to stop you seeing them?' Miranda said. 'You could have been hurt.'

Holly shook her head. 'That as well,' she said 'But what I want to know right now is what Peter was doing sneaking back into the library.'

'Peter!' said Miranda. 'Have you been holding out on us?'

Peter ran a hand through his hair. 'Not exactly,' he said. He looked at Mr Granville, who had started picking up bits of the suit of armour. 'Look,' he said. 'Let's help get this mess cleared up and go somewhere private to talk about it.'

'OK,' said Holly. 'But I warn you, no answer, no pooling!'

'Too right,' said Miranda as she led the way into the hall. 'You've got a bit of explaining to do, Peter!'

Attack in the night

'In here,' said Miranda, leading the way into the girls' room.

Both girls turned towards Peter and stared at him.

'OK, OK,' said Peter, 'I admit it. I went back to the library.'

'Why?' said Holly.

Peter grinned at her. 'To see if I could find the clue you had found,' he said.

'What clue?' said Miranda.

'Aha!' said Peter, grinning at her.

'And did you find it?' said Holly to Peter.

Peter nodded. 'It took a while for the penny to drop,' he said. 'But I got there at last.'

'I don't know what took you so long,' Holly said. 'After all, you loaned me the book.'

'*The Inside-Out Clue*?' said Peter.

Miranda put her hands on her hips and

faced the other two. 'Will somebody please tell me what's going on?' she demanded.

Holly was still looking suspiciously at Peter. 'Peter will,' she said.

Peter shook his head. 'You've got a suspicious mind, Holly Adams,' he said.

Miranda was dancing up and down with impatience. 'I'm going to scream in a minute,' she said.

'Don't do that,' said Peter hastily. He looked at Holly. 'It was the window,' he said. 'There was no broken glass in the room.' He paused. 'But there was broken glass in the flowerbed outside. Just like in the book I loaned Holly. The clue was inside-out!'

Miranda looked puzzled, then her face cleared. 'Oh, I get it,' she said. 'If the glass was on the outside then the window was broken from the inside.' Then her face fell. 'But how does that help us? We still haven't eliminated one another. I mean, one of us could have been outside.'

'But I wouldn't have gone back to the library if I'd thrown the brick,' said Peter.

'True,' said Miranda. Then she turned to

Holly. 'So why did you keep watch on the library?' she said.

'Because I saw you pick up that piece of paper and I wanted to see if the person who dropped it came back for it,' said Holly.

'But according to Mr Granville, that bit of paper has nothing to do with the murder mystery,' said Miranda. 'So that doesn't get us anywhere.'

Peter frowned. 'I reckon the only way to eliminate one another is to stick close together,' he said. 'That way, when the murder is committed, we'll be able to give one another alibis.'

'Good thinking,' said Miranda. 'What do you think, Holly?'

Holly sat down on her bed and looked thoughtful. 'I think I'd like to have a look at that bit of paper you picked up,' she said to Miranda.

'OK,' said Miranda. 'But you won't be able to make any sense of it. It's just a lot of lines.'

Miranda spread the paper out on Holly's bed and the Mystery Kids pored over it.

'It does look a bit like geometry homework,' said Peter.

'It could be some kind of plan,' said Holly.

'A plan of what?' said Peter. 'A drainage system? It isn't like any of the plans Dad draws.'

'Maybe it's a map,' Miranda suggested.

'Or maybe somebody was just doodling,' said Holly, picking the paper up and turning it round. 'It doesn't seem to make any sense no matter which way up you hold it.' She gave the paper back to Miranda. Miranda put it down on the table between their beds.

'I'm whacked,' said Peter. 'I think I'll go to bed and try and work out who threw that brick.' He frowned. 'Did anybody else come back to the library, Holly?'

Holly nodded. 'Mark went in for a book and Mr Thomson went in, wandered around and went out again.'

'But why would the person who threw the brick want to go back to the library in the first place?' said Miranda. 'It doesn't make sense.'

'Nothing makes sense to me at the moment,' Peter said. 'I'm going to bed.'

'Me too,' said Miranda as Peter closed the door behind him. 'How about you, Holly?'

'Mmm,' said Holly. 'In a minute.'

Holly sat for a while staring out of the window at the lawn in front of the house. It was nearly dark now and she could barely make out the outline of the maze.

'Oh, I'm tired too,' she said at last. 'My mind is just a jumble of things.'

'Maybe sleeping will sort them out,' Miranda said as she got into bed. 'Goodnight.'

Holly smiled. Then she remembered what the note round the brick had said. 'I shall kill. Will it be tonight? Be on your guard.'

Would the murderer strike tonight? And who would be the victim? And who, Holly wondered, had knocked that suit of armour over? Who was the spy?

Holly woke up. At once she was alert, listening. Something, some sixth sense, told her not to move. Someone was in the room and it wasn't Miranda. Miranda was asleep, breathing steadily.

Holly stared into the darkness, letting her eyes roll from side to side. Was that a movement by the window? No, it was only the curtain blowing slightly in the breeze. She forced herself to breathe normally. Then she saw it. A shadow, massive and black against the deeper darkness of the far wall. It moved towards the door, opened it, and was gone. Holly wanted to call out but she forced herself to be silent until she was sure it was safe to move. She listened to the sounds in the room. Nothing but her own breathing and Miranda's.

Quietly, Holly slid out of bed and padded to the bedroom door. She put her ear against it but she couldn't hear anything. She opened the door and, moving slowly, crept along the corridor, staying close to the wall. She looked over the gallery at the hall below.

Moonlight played over the black and white squares and shone dully on the suits of armour. Holly gasped. Did one of the suits of armour move or was it only a trick of the light? Holly peered more closely at them. Were they really all just suits of armour? Could one of those be a real man, the man who had been in their room?

She headed for the staircase, her feet making no sound on the thick carpet. Just before she got to the top, she hesitated and sank down behind the stair rails, peering through them, listening. Then she screwed her eyes up and searched the shadows below her. There *was* somebody down there, half-way down the stairs. Holly could just make out a dark shape flattened against the wall. She was watching the figure on the stairs so closely, she didn't hear the steps behind her until a voice whispered in her ear.

'What are you up to?'

The breath stopped in her throat and her heart hammered against her ribs. She whirled round. It was Miranda.

'Cripes!' she whispered. 'Don't *do* that, Miranda!'

'What's up?' Miranda said.

'Shh,' said Holly. 'There's somebody down there.'

But it was too late. Miranda's piercing whisper had alerted whoever was there. Somebody moved in the hall below.

'Quick!' Holly said, making for the stairs.

Miranda was beside her as she hurtled

down the stairs and straight into somebody.

'Ouch!' said a voice she recognised.

'Peter!' cried Holly. 'What on earth are you doing here?'

'Same as you I guess,' he said. 'I heard a noise and got up to see who it was.'

'There's something going on down there,' said Holly.

'Let's put a light on,' Miranda whispered.

'We don't know where the switches are,' said Peter. 'Just keep quiet.'

Slowly, the three of them crept down the stairs. From the hallway below came the sound of a scuffle.

'Two of them,' Peter said. 'Come on!'

There was a crack and a groan and then a thump that made Holly's heart turn over. Then the three of them were racing for the hall. Below them a door swung open and closed again. The green baize door at the end of the hall. Holly caught a glimpse of a dark figure disappearing through it. She couldn't tell if it was the man who had been in her room. She couldn't even tell if this figure was a man or a woman. She made a dash for the hall. She was at the bottom of the stairs when her foot caught on something soft and she nearly fell. Peter grabbed her.

'Stop!' he said urgently.

Holly stopped, her heart hammering. 'What is it?' she said.

But she knew what it was. She had nearly tripped over a body.

Then relief flooded through her. It was all part of the murder mystery. They had interrupted the murderer. Now at least they would find out who the victim was.

'Hang on,' said Peter. 'I've found a light switch.'

At once the hall was flooded with light, illuminating the body lying awkwardly across the bottom step.

'Mr Granville?' said Holly. 'He's the victim?'

'I didn't think that would be allowed,' said Miranda. 'After all, Mr Granville is the Mystery Master.'

Peter bent over the body then looked up at them, his face serious. 'I don't think it *is* allowed,' he said. 'And I don't think we're dealing with the murder mystery here.' His voice sounded strained. 'This is for real,' he said. 'Somebody has just attacked him!'

A ball of string

'Maybe he just tripped,' Miranda said, her voice trembling.

'Mr Granville,' said Holly, getting down on her knees beside him. She looked at Peter and Miranda. 'You don't think he's dead, do you?' she said.

Miranda laid her ear against Mr Granville's mouth. 'He's breathing,' she said.

Peter looked round. 'Shouldn't we call an ambulance or something?' he said.

Mr Granville stirred and opened his eyes.

'Oh,' said Holly, relief flooding through her. 'Are you all right, Mr Granville? What happened? Did you fall down the stairs?'

Mr Granville sat up shakily and put a hand to his head. 'Fall?' he said. 'No, I didn't fall. I was pushed!' He fingered the back of his head. 'Ow!' he said. 'And whoever shoved me gave me a crack on the head for good measure, I think. It certainly feels like it.'

'Pushed?' said Miranda. 'Who would do a thing like that?'

'That settles it,' said Peter. 'I'll ring the police. There could be a burglar in the house!'

'No, no, don't do that,' Mr Granville said, sitting up and wincing again.

Holly looked at him. 'But somebody pushed you down the stairs. You'll have to tell the police. What if there is a burglar loose?'

Mr Granville sighed. 'Look,' he said. 'I might not be thinking very straight at the moment but I know one thing. The people here have come for a nice safe mystery weekend – one where nobody really gets murdered and nobody really gets hurt. If they hear about this they'll leave and the word will get round.' He looked at the Mystery Kids seriously. 'We need these weekends to keep the place going,' he said. 'We can't afford to frighten the guests away.'

The Mystery Kids looked at one another. What Mr Granville said made sense.

'I can imagine what Mrs Partridge would say,' Peter said.

Miranda nodded. Mrs Partridge seemed to have an opinion about everything. 'She would have a fit! And Mrs Martin is nervous enough already. She would have her bags packed right away,' she said.

'What were you doing down here anyway?' Holly said to Mr Granville. 'Did you hear something?'

Mr Granville smiled ruefully. 'I was laying clues for the mystery,' he said.

'Maybe one of the guests got too enthusiastic and followed you, thinking you were the murderer,' Peter said.

'And knocked you over by accident,' said Miranda.

'And hit him on the head by accident?' Holly said.

Miranda's face fell.

'Look, Mr Granville,' Peter said. 'Maybe you should inform the police. I mean, you could have been really badly hurt.'

'What will Mrs Granville say?' Holly said.

'She'll say, "What on earth is going on

here?"' said a voice behind them. 'Do you want to wake the whole house?'

Holly, Peter and Miranda moved and Mrs Granville caught sight of her husband.

'James,' she cried, running down the stairs towards them.

'It's all right,' Mr Granville said. 'I'm fine, Pat.'

Holly, Peter and Miranda moved away while Mr Granville explained to his wife what had happened. They watched her lead him slowly into the lounge, asking questions in a soft voice.

'Right,' said Miranda. 'Let's get to work.'

'What?' said Holly.

'Clues,' Miranda said. 'And real ones. This is a real mystery.'

Peter looked round the floor. 'Did either of you see anything?' he said.

Holly pursed her lips, eyes searching the hall. 'I thought I saw somebody run away,' she said. 'Through that baize door at the end of the hall.'

'If I remember the plan of the house, that leads to the kitchens and the back stairs,' said Peter.

'Oh, terrific,' said Miranda. 'That means whoever it is could be anywhere by now. You can get to every part of the house by those stairs.'

'Was it a man or a woman?' Peter asked.

Holly shook her head. 'I couldn't tell,' she said. She looked round. 'With all this armour it was hard to tell which of the figures were real.'

Miranda nodded then she made a dive under a heavy wooden chair. 'Look,' she said.

'It's only a ball of string,' Peter said. 'It could have been there for ages.'

Miranda looked superior. 'It may be a ball of string to you,' she said. 'But to me it's exhibit A. The first clue. You heard Mrs Granville say how clean Mrs Billings keeps the place. She wouldn't have left a ball of string lying around.'

'And look,' said Holly. She bent and picked up a small glass bottle.

'It's some of that bath oil Mrs Granville makes,' Peter said.

Holly looked at the label. 'Lavender, geranium and marjoram,' she read out. 'Mrs

Granville said she put the last of these in the bedrooms this weekend.'

Peter looked at her. 'So?' he said.

Holly's face flushed with excitement. 'Don't you see?' she said. 'If they were all in the bedrooms yesterday, what's this one doing here in the hall tonight?'

'I get it,' Miranda said. 'Whoever pushed Mr Granville downstairs must have brought it down.'

'But why on earth would anyone do that?' said Peter.

'It doesn't matter why they did it,' said Holly. 'But it does mean that whoever pushed Mr Granville is a guest.'

Holly, Peter and Miranda turned. Mrs Granville was coming out of the lounge, her arm supporting Mr Granville. He still looked a bit shaky.

'Maybe James is right,' Mrs Granville said to them. 'It's only a bump on the head so I don't think we need to call a doctor.' She looked upwards towards the bedrooms. 'Thank goodness this house is so large,' she said. 'We don't seem to have disturbed anyone else.'

'But what about the police?' said Holly. 'Don't you think we should call them?'

Mrs Granville bit her lip. 'I think James is right about that too,' she said. 'A fun mystery is one thing but a real one is quite another. We really can't afford to have the guests upset by police questioning.' She looked at her husband. 'I've had a quick look around and nothing seems to be missing.'

Mr Granville patted her hand. 'It was probably just one of the guests getting over-enthusiastic about the clues I was laying,' he said. 'Maybe they bumped into me and ran away because they were embarrassed. I'm probably imagining somebody pushed me. That crack on the head could have happened when I fell down.'

Mrs Granville smiled but she still looked a little worried. 'And now I think I'd better get you upstairs, James,' she said. She turned to the Mystery Kids. 'I certainly can't see what burglars would be after,' she said. 'We haven't got anything of any real value – not now.' She smiled at them. 'You three get back to bed now,' she said. 'And thanks for your help. If it was a burglar, I reckon you scared him away.'

Holly, Peter and Miranda watched as she led Mr Granville upstairs. They followed more slowly and went into the girls' room.

'Why didn't you tell her about the string and the oil?' Miranda said to Holly.

Holly looked at Miranda. 'Why didn't you?' she said.

Miranda shrugged. 'I don't know. I suppose I didn't want to worry her any more. I mean it looks like one of the guests was down there, doesn't it?'

Holly frowned. 'I agree,' she said. 'And it would explain how the oil got there. But what about the string? What was that doing there?'

Miranda shrugged. 'Anybody could have left a ball of string lying around,' she said. 'There wasn't anything special about it, was there?'

'I don't think so,' said Holly slowly. 'I didn't look at it too closely. Where is it?'

Miranda looked at her. 'Haven't you got it?' she said.

Holly shook her head. 'I thought you had the string *and* the oil,' she replied.

The girls looked at Peter but he shook

his head too. 'We must have left them downstairs,' he said. 'We can't go back down now.'

'We can look at them in the morning,' Holly said. 'But I'm sure there was nothing strange about that string.'

'It's the oil that worries me,' said Peter. 'It means that a guest attacked Mr Granville. And in some ways that's more worrying than a burglar.'

'I suppose so,' said Holly.

Miranda frowned. 'One thing's for sure,' she said. 'Whoever it is is a real weirdo.'

'What makes you say that?' Peter asked.

Miranda looked at him. 'A ball of string and a bottle of oil,' she said. 'Why on earth would anybody go wandering around the house in the middle of the night carrying those things?'

But Holly wasn't listening. She was scrabbling around on the floor beside the bedside table.

'What are you doing down there?' Peter said.

Holly looked up. 'I'll tell you something else that's mysterious,' she said. 'Miranda left that piece of paper with the design on it on the bedside table.'

'So?' said Peter.

'It isn't here now,' said Holly. She pushed a lock of hair out of her eyes and stood up. 'And I've just remembered what woke me up in the first place.' She looked at the other two. 'Somebody was in our room,' she said. 'And it looks like whoever it was took that piece of paper.' She took a deep breath. 'And I'm willing to bet it was the same person that pushed Mr Granville down the stairs!'

The Mystery Kids looked at one another.

'Just how many mysteries are going on at Granville Towers this weekend?' Miranda said.

7 Murder!

'So what we've got to do is get the real mystery sorted out from the fun one,' Holly said to Peter and Miranda on their way down to breakfast next morning.

'We need to give the mysteries names,' said Peter.

'The Murder Mystery is all right,' said Holly. 'It's the other one we need a name for.'

'"The Mysterious Bath Oil Bashing"?' said Miranda.

Holly gave her a dig in the ribs. 'Poor Mr Granville,' she said. 'I wonder how he's feeling this morning.'

'I was so tired last night, it didn't quite sink in,' said Peter to Miranda. 'That paper you found in the library has got to be part of the Bath Oil Bashing Mystery.'

'How do you make that out?' said Miranda.

'Because I think Holly is right,' said Peter. 'Whoever attacked Mr Granville also stole the diagram.'

'You can't know that for certain,' Miranda said.

Holly nodded her head firmly. 'I'm sure of it,' she said. 'The only other people around were Mr and Mrs Granville. Besides, Mr Granville says the diagram isn't part of the murder mystery.' She frowned. 'Who knew we had that paper?'

'Mr Granville,' said Miranda.

'And someone else,' said Peter. 'Don't you remember? There was somebody outside the door when you showed it to Mr Granville.'

'But we don't know who that someone was,' said Holly. 'I reckon it was the same person who attacked Mr Granville.' She shivered. 'I wouldn't like to think of more than one person wandering about Granville Towers listening at doors and bopping people on the head.'

Miranda nodded. 'Make sure you lock your door,' she said to Peter. 'At Granville Towers, anything can happen!' Then she froze as a sound ripped through the air. 'What on earth was that?'

'It was another scream,' said Peter.

'And this time it wasn't a peacock,' Holly added. 'It came from the dining-room!'

The three raced down the rest of the stairs, across the hall and into the dining-room.

Mrs Partridge was standing there, her hands to her mouth.

'It isn't real, Edna,' little Mr Partridge was saying. 'Pull yourself together. It's the murder mystery.'

Mrs Partridge began to calm down. 'Oh, but it gave me such a fright, Joe,' she said, her large frame quivering. 'It looks so real.'

'Oh, my goodness,' said a voice at the door. Holly turned to see Mrs Martin clutching Mr Martin's arm.

'It's the murder,' said Mr Martin. 'I must say it looks pretty good.'

'Oh, Jeremy, it's so gruesome!' said Mrs Martin.

Mr Martin coughed and patted her hand. 'Sorry, dear,' he said.

Holly looked at the dining-room table.

Sprawled across it was a man's body. Sticking out of his back was the handle of a bread knife.

'Ugh!' she said. She shivered. 'It is just pretend, isn't it?'

Peter grinned. 'Of course it is,' he said. He put his head to one side. 'I didn't expect that,' he said.

'What?' said Miranda, staring in fascination at the body.

'A bread knife,' said Peter. 'I mean the house is full of swords and daggers and guns and stuff.'

Miranda giggled and Holly began to feel better. It had been a shock to see someone else sprawled out even though this one was very definitely pretend.

'Let's hope it's a trick knife,' Mark said, coming into the dining-room. He looked at the body critically. 'The blood looks good, doesn't it?'

Mr Partridge had gone over to the body and was examining it.

'It's Mr Thomson,' he said. 'And he's making a really good corpse. You can hardly believe he's not really dead.'

Holly's breath caught. Mr Thomson's face was turned towards them, the eyes closed. As she watched, his eyes opened and he gave Mr Partridge a distinctly chilly look.

Holly giggled in relief. It was certainly reassuring to know he was only acting.

'Clues,' she said briskly. 'We mustn't move the body.'

'What body?' said Miss Finch from the doorway. Her eyes glinted from behind their half-moon spectacles. 'Oh, it's happened!' she cried. She clasped her hands to her throat and took hold of a couple of scarves. 'Quite right, Holly. Don't anybody move anything until we've looked for all the clues!'

Soon the dining-room was swarming with sleuths noting down clues.

'He's knocked over a clock,' said Miss Finch, her glasses halfway down her nose in her excitement. 'It stopped at eight fifteen but that could be a red herring.'

'And his boiled egg is still warm,' Mrs Martin said shyly, looking at the uneaten egg in front of Mr Thomson.

'Oh, look!' said Miranda. 'He's spilled some sugar and he tried to write in it.'

Everybody crowded round.

'It looks like an "M",' said Peter.

'"M" for Martin,' said Mr Partridge.

'Or Mark,' said Mr Martin, fingering his beard.

'Or Miranda,' Holly said with a grin. But she knew this couldn't be the case; Miranda had been with her and Peter the whole time.

'Or maybe it's "M" for murder,' said Miss Finch. 'Although if he was stabbed in the back, it was hardly likely to be an accident!' The Granvilles were the last to arrive and Holly was glad to see that Mr Granville was looking well.

'Don't you worry about me,' he whispered when he saw her concerned expression. 'I'm as fit as a fiddle now.' He smiled. 'And thanks for last night.'

Then he became brisk, the Mystery Master again, while Mrs Granville went off to get Mrs Billings and organise breakfast. At last the Granvilles took the 'body' away. Holly held the door open for them and Miranda scurried up.

'Do you think Mr Thomson will give us an

interview for the school magazine?' she said to Mrs Granville. 'I've never met a real writer before.'

'I'm sure he will if you ask him,' Mrs Granville replied.

Holly shrugged. 'He should,' she said. 'He'll have plenty of time now he's a corpse.'

Miranda giggled. 'Why did the skeleton never do any work?' she said.

Holly grinned. 'Why?'

Miranda looked at them. 'Because he was bone idle,' she said.

'That's terrible,' said Holly.

Miranda nodded. 'Isn't it?' she said.

'I would hate to be the victim,' Peter said. 'I'd much rather be a detective.'

Mrs Granville smiled. 'Mr Thomson rather wanted to be the victim,' she said. 'He told us it would give him more time to research his book; to find out how people went about solving the murder, that kind of thing.'

'I suppose so,' said Miranda. 'But I still think solving a mystery must be much more exciting than writing one.'

Mrs Granville's eyes twinkled. 'Have you got all the clues?' she asked.

Miranda nodded. 'I hope sc,' she said.

'First of all we'll have to find out who has alibis,' Holly said. Then she smiled. 'Oh, I've just realised. We've done it.'

'What?' said Miranda.

'We've given one another alibis,' said Holly. 'We've eliminated ourselves.'

'That's right,' said Peter. 'We've been together since before eight o'clock. So if the clock in the dining-room really did stop at the time of the murder we're in the clear.'

'Terrific!' said Miranda. She turned to Mrs Granville. 'We're so used to working on mysteries together. It was weird to suspect each other,' she said.

Holly gave a sigh of relief. 'I'm glad we don't have to work separately any longer,' she said.

Miranda's face lit up. 'So am I. But right now, I'm starving. After breakfast I vote we do a bit of investigating then meet up and pool all our clues.'

'Agreed,' said Holly.

'Sounds a good idea to me,' said Peter. 'Especially the bit about breakfast.'

* * *

'The clock clue is OK,' said Miranda later that morning, plonking herself down on the lawn beside Holly and Peter. 'It wasn't a red herring.'

'How do you know?' said Holly.

Miranda grinned. 'I asked Mrs Billings. She was in the dining-room laying the table. She heard the clock chime eight. She says she must have been in there for about ten minutes after that.' Miranda paused. 'And she saw Mr Thomson coming downstairs as she went back into the kitchen,' she finished.

'Right,' said Holly. 'Let's pool our clues. What have we got?'

'I spoke to Mrs Billings as well,' Peter said, consulting his notebook. 'And she says Mr Thomson didn't go straight into the dining-room. Somebody called to him from upstairs and he turned to wait for that person.'

'But Mrs Billings didn't see who it was?' said Holly.

Peter shook his head. 'She was in a hurry to get back to the kitchen. She couldn't even remember whether it was a man or a woman.'

'Miss Finch was in the garden,' Holly said.

'Did anybody see her?' Miranda asked.

Holly nodded. 'Mr Partridge says he did. He was looking out of his bedroom window.'

'Where was Mrs Partridge?' said Peter.

'She had gone downstairs,' said Holly.

'And she found the body. That's *always* suspicious,' said Peter.

'We can forget about Mr Thomson,' said Miranda. 'You can't stick a knife in your own back.'

'So who has an alibi so far?' said Peter.

'We do,' said Miranda.

'Mr Thomson,' said Holly.

'Miss Finch,' said Miranda. 'Mr Partridge saw her in the garden.'

'Did Miss Finch see Mr Partridge?' said Peter. 'After all, he could have seen her from the dining-room.'

Holly made a note. 'We'll ask her,' she said.

Miranda giggled. 'I wish we could just interview Mr Thomson and ask him who did it,' she said. She looked at her notebook. 'So who is left on the list of suspects?' she said.

Peter read out the names. 'Mark, Mrs Partridge and the Martins.'

'I keep forgetting about the Martins. They're so quiet,' said Holly.

'The perfect suspects,' said Peter. 'I'll take them.'

'I'll take Mrs Partridge,' said Miranda.

'And I'll take Mark,' said Holly.

'Don't forget Mr Partridge,' said Miranda. 'We have to check his alibi with Miss Finch.'

'They can't all have alibis,' Holly said. 'One of them must be the murderer.'

Peter and Miranda nodded.

'One more thing,' said Peter, looking serious.

'What?' said Holly.

Peter looked at the girls. 'I don't think Mr Granville really believes his attack was an accident,' he said. 'I know *I* don't.'

'Nor me,' said Miranda. Holly nodded her agreement.

'So while we're checking out alibis for this morning,' Peter went on, 'let's try and find out if anybody was wandering around the house last night.'

'Or if anybody lost a ball of string,' said Holly.

'Oh!' said Miranda. 'I forgot to say. I had

a look for the string and the oil in the hall after breakfast – and they weren't there. They'd gone.'

'Maybe Mrs Billings tidied them away,' said Peter.

Holly looked at the other two. 'Or maybe the attacker came back for the evidence,' she said. 'I think Peter's right. We've got to find out who was on the prowl last night!'

The murderer!

'Who can we eliminate now?' Holly said that evening.

It was after dinner and the Mystery Kids had spent the day, notebooks in hand, checking up on everyone's movements. Now they were sitting on the lawn in front of the house.

'I didn't get anywhere asking people about last night,' said Peter.

Miranda pulled a face. 'Neither did I,' she said. 'I mean where would you expect a person to be in the middle of the night except in bed? I can tell you I felt pretty strange asking everybody how they'd slept and if they'd had a bath.'

Holly giggled. 'You certainly annoyed Mrs Partridge when you asked her how much of her bath oil she'd used.'

Miranda grinned and pursed up her mouth. '"Well, really, I didn't know it was rationed!"' she mimicked.

'I started to ask everybody if I could borrow some string,' said Peter.

'And?' said Holly.

'Mark got some for me,' he replied. 'But it wasn't the same kind as the stuff we found.'

Holly looked thoughtfully at the other two. 'You know, there's something funny about Mark,' she said. 'I've felt it from the start but I don't know what it is.'

'Intuition is no good without evidence,' Miranda stated loftily. 'I think I read that somewhere. What you need are facts.'

'And we haven't got any facts about what people were up to last night,' said Peter.

'OK,' said Holly. 'If we can't find out who bashed Mr Granville over the head, at least can we solve the murder mystery? How did you two get on with the alibis?'

'The Martins have an alibi,' Peter said. 'Mark says he saw them coming into the house as he was going out at eight fifteen.'

'Going out?' said Miranda. 'Where was he going?'

Holly looked at her notebook. 'According to Mark he was going for a walk before breakfast,' she said.

Miranda's eyes narrowed as she consulted her notebook. 'I was checking up on Mrs Partridge. Mrs Martin said Mrs Partridge was going into the dining-room just as they came in the front door from the garden.'

Holly chewed the tip of her pencil. 'So the Martins can give Mrs Partridge an alibi,' she said.

'And Mark can give the Martins an alibi,' said Peter.

'What about Mr Partridge?' said Miranda.

'Oh, I checked that,' said Peter. 'Miss Finch did see him.'

Holly looked at the other two. 'But that's impossible,' she said. 'They can't all have alibis.'

Peter and Miranda looked crestfallen. 'We must have missed something,' said Peter.

Holly frowned. 'The question is *what*,' she said.

Miranda shook her head. 'It all checks out,' she said running her eye down the list of suspects. She gazed across the lawns.

'Maybe it was a peacock that did it. I haven't checked their alibis.'

Holly giggled then turned her head to look outside. 'There's Mr Thomson,' she said as a dark figure came into view round the side of the maze.

'What if we just ask him?' Miranda said.

'No,' Peter said firmly. 'We can't ask the victim.'

'But I could see if he'd give me that interview,' Miranda said. She sprang up and scurried off to intercept Mr Thomson.

Holly and Peter watched Miranda approach Mr Thomson. They saw her exchange words with the fellow guest. Then he turned on his heels and strode towards the side of the house. Miranda was left standing in the middle of the lawn looking after Mr Thomson. Then she turned back to Holly and Peter, shoulders sagging. She was clearly disappointed.

'What did he say?' said Peter.

Miranda shook her head. 'He says he'll give me an interview tomorrow,' she said, sitting down beside them.

'Why not now?' said Holly.

Miranda shrugged. 'He says he hasn't done enough work on his book yet.' She snorted. 'If you ask me it won't be a mystery book anyway. It'll be a gardening book.'

'What?' said Peter.

Miranda looked at him. 'Didn't you see the state of him?' she said. 'He looked as if he'd just crawled through a hedge backwards.'

Holly looked thoughtfully at the maze. 'You don't think he could have been in there, do you?' she said.

Miranda shrugged. 'Maybe,' she said. 'Maybe his mystery book is set in a maze. Maybe he was in there for research.'

'At least he didn't get lost,' said Peter. 'That's all we need. A murder mystery where all the suspects have alibis, Mr Granville attacked in the middle of the night and a guest lost in the maze.'

'But he didn't get lost,' said Miranda.

Holly narrowed her eyes. 'Then he must have a very good sense of direction.' She turned to the others. 'Meanwhile, we have just got to break one of these alibis. I mean somebody has to be the murderer!'

* * *

But on Sunday morning on the way down to breakfast they were just as puzzled.

'Wonderful morning,' Mr Martin called from the hall below.

Holly looked down. Mr Martin was just coming in the front door. As he came in, he stood aside to let Mr Partridge pass by. Something jogged Holly's memory as she watched the little scene.

'Where's your notebook, Miranda?' she said.

Miranda pulled out her notebook. 'What are you looking for?' she said.

But Holly was counting off on her fingers. 'Twice,' she muttered. 'You have to double check.'

'What?' said Peter.

'Come along, you three,' said Miss Finch's cheerful voice as she passed them by on the stairs, scarves fluttering. 'Time to hand in your answers.'

But the Mystery Kids were engrossed in Miranda's notebook.

'Just coming, Miss Finch,' Holly said absently.

'Double check,' said Peter. 'Of course.'

Miranda was muttering away. 'Miss Finch and Mr Partridge.'

'Mrs Partridge and the Martins,' Peter said.

Then they looked up from the notebook and stared at one another. 'Mark and the Martins. It doesn't check out,' said Holly. 'Not both ways.'

'Mark's alibi,' Miranda said. 'He gave the Martins an alibi but the Martins didn't give *him* an alibi!'

'And we nearly missed it,' said Peter.

'Nearly,' said Miranda. 'I'll bet we're right.'

'We must be,' said Holly. 'There's no other solution. We've found the murderer.'

Breakfast was over and Mr Granville was ready to make the announcement. Before him on the table were the envelopes everyone had handed in. Everybody held their breath as he opened one envelope after another. Then he smiled. 'We have one correct solution.'

The detectives looked at one another. Mr Granville cleared his throat and looked round the table. 'Would the murderer please stand up?' he said.

For a moment no one moved, then a figure got slowly to his feet. Mark.

'We were right,' said Peter.

Mark grinned. 'And I thought I had you fooled,' he said.

Holly grinned back at him. 'You nearly did,' she said. 'You were really clever about that alibi you gave the Martins.'

'It was only when we realised that the Martins hadn't given *you* an alibi that we realised you were the only one we couldn't double check on,' Miranda said.

Mr Granville smiled. 'The first rule of detection,' he said. 'Never believe anything you can't double check.'

'I thought it was Mr Martin,' said Miss Finch ruefully. 'I think the beard made me suspicious!'

Mr Martin laughed. 'And I thought it was Mrs Partridge,' he said. 'After all, she found the body.'

'Well done, Mark,' said Mr Partridge. 'You covered your tracks well. At least as far as the rest of us were concerned.'

Mark smiled and looked slightly embarrassed. 'Actually,' he said, 'I've done it before.'

'What?' said Mrs Martin.

Mrs Granville looked round her guests. 'Mark is our younger son,' she said. 'Usually we use actors for the victim and murderer but they let us down this weekend.' She turned to Mr Thomson. 'Luckily Mr Thomson offered to be the victim and Mark always stands in for us when there is an emergency.'

'Of course,' Holly said. 'You knew where the library was without the plan of the house. When we first heard the window break, you said straight away that the sound had come from the library!'

'Wow!' said Mark. 'You really are a supersleuth, aren't you?'

'Not that super,' said Holly ruefully, 'or I'd have got it at the time.' Then she shook her head. 'And I *should* have noticed how like your father you are. No wonder Mr Granville reminded me of someone. It was you!'

'But you nearly let slip that we had a pile of mystery books in the library,' Mrs Granville said to her son.

'I didn't even notice that,' said Peter.

'I think he did brilliantly!' Miranda said.

'How about a round of applause for the Mystery Kids and the murderer?' said Mr Martin. He looked round. 'Not forgetting the victim of course,' he added.

But Mr Thomson was halfway to the door. 'I think I'll just take a little walk,' he said.

'Oh, hang on a minute,' Miranda said. She caught Mr Thomson just as he was making for the door. 'What about my interview?' she asked.

Mr Thomson looked annoyed. 'What interview?' he said impatiently.

'The interview about writing mysteries,' Miranda said.

'We wouldn't take up much of your time,' Holly put in as she and Peter came up to stand beside Miranda.

Mr Thomson smiled thinly and walked out into the hall. 'If you're quick, then,' he said. 'I haven't got all day, you know. I'm a busy man. I've got my notes to write up before I leave.'

'For your book,' Miranda said. 'Of course. What's it going to be called?'

Mr Thomson scratched his head. 'I haven't decided on a title yet,' he said.

Miranda frowned. 'What's it about then?' she said.

Mr Thomson looked even more impatient. He looked out of the dining-room windows, across the lawns. 'It's about a jewellery robbery,' he said.

Holly smiled. 'How exciting,' she said. 'There was a jewellery robbery here at Granville Towers years ago.'

Mr Thomson turned to her. 'What do you know about that?' he said.

Holly drew back. 'Nothing much. But the disappearance of the Granville Treasure is one of the most mysterious unsolved crimes ever.'

Mr Thomson put a hand in his pocket, pulled out his handkerchief and blew his nose. 'Lot of nonsense,' he said. 'The family probably arranged it for the insurance money.'

'The Granvilles would never do that,' Miranda blurted out. 'They're far too nice. Aren't they, Peter?'

But Peter wasn't listening. 'What?' he said.

'Peter!' said Holly.

Peter looked at Mr Thomson. 'Sorry,' he said. 'Maybe we shouldn't bother you. As you said, you're a busy man.'

Mr Thomson looked at Peter in surprise. Then he shrugged. 'I'm glad to see one of you has a bit of sense,' he said unpleasantly.

And with that he walked away.

'Well,' said Miranda. 'What a rude man! And thanks a lot, Peter! You just lost us our interview.'

Holly was staring after Mr Thomson with a frown on her face.

'There's something very odd about Mr Thomson,' she said.

'You mean apart from being the rudest man on earth?' said Miranda.

Holly nodded. 'Remember you spoke to him the other day? Didn't you say he doesn't know the first thing about mystery books?' she said.

Miranda looked thoughtful. 'That's right,' she said. 'I kept mentioning books and he didn't recognise a single one.' She bit her lip. 'But he did know about the jewellery theft years ago – that was obvious.' She thought for a moment. 'Maybe he's an undercover crime reporter,' she said. 'Maybe that's why he's here.'

'But that mystery is years old,' said Holly.

'What if he's from the insurance company?' Miranda said. Her eyes grew round. 'You don't think the Granvilles really did have a hand in that robbery, do you?'

'If they had the jewels they wouldn't have had to turn the house into a hotel,' said Holly. 'You heard Mr Granville say so.'

Miranda thought for a moment, then shook her head. 'If there really was suspicion about them, then they wouldn't be able to sell the jewels,' she said. 'It would be too obvious if they suddenly had a heap of money.'

But Holly shook her head. 'Well, I think if anybody is suspicious around here it's Mr Thomson.'

'Oh, he's suspicious all right,' said Peter.

'Well, what do you know? He talks!' said Miranda, still annoyed at Peter.

'I couldn't get a word in,' said Peter. 'Didn't you see what was in his pocket?'

'No,' said Holly. 'What?'

'When he pulled his handkerchief out a piece of paper slipped halfway out with it.'

'And?' Miranda asked eagerly, forgetting to be annoyed.

'And it was the diagram,' Peter said. 'The one you found in the library. The one that was stolen from your room.' Peter looked seriously at the girls. 'Mr Thomson isn't a mystery writer. It's all a sham!' he said.

'He must have been the one listening outside the door when we showed the paper to Mr Granville,' said Miranda.

'And it must have been Mr Thomson who came into our room the night Mr Granville was attacked,' Holly said.

Miranda nodded furiously. 'That means he was wandering about the house that night,' she said.

'Which means he probably attacked Mr Granville,' Holly added. She frowned. 'Which room is his?'

Peter narrowed his eyes. 'What are you planning?' he said.

'I was wondering whether he had a bottle of bath oil in his room,' she said.

'We all have,' said Miranda.

'We all *had* one,' said Holly. 'But we know a bottle went missing from one of the rooms.'

Peter and Miranda looked at her. 'You mean we should search his room?' said Miranda.

Holly nodded. 'If there is a bottle of oil there then he's just an unpleasant individual but if there isn't . . .'

'It wouldn't prove he attacked Mr Granville,' said Peter.

'But it would make it a real possibility,' said Holly.

Peter nodded. 'It would certainly be suspicious,' he said.

'Where did Mr Thomson go?' said Miranda.

Holly nodded in the direction of the gardens. 'Down there somewhere,' she said. 'The coast will be clear.'

'What are we waiting for?' said Miranda. 'Let's go!'

The maze

Mrs Billings was cleaning the bedrooms. The doors of all the rooms along the corridor stood open and a vacuum was buzzing somewhere as they crept into Mr Thomson's room. His suitcase was standing ready at the bottom of his bed.

'Looks like he's ready for a quick getaway,' said Miranda.

Holly frowned as she searched the bathroom. 'There's no bath oil in here,' she said.

'Hurry up,' Peter said from the door. 'The vacuum's stopped.'

Holly turned and caught the view of the lawns from Mr Thomson's window. Mr Thomson was walking towards the maze. What was he doing down there when he was supposed to be writing up his notes? Something flashed into Holly's mind.

'Come on, Holly!' Miranda cried and Holly lost her train of thought.

'Will you two get out of there?' Peter called from the door. 'Mrs Billings is coming!'

Holly moved towards the door. Then she noticed a patch of dirt on the carpet. Mrs Billings obviously hadn't done this room yet. She looked at it. It was leaf mould – the same kind of stuff that Peter had got on his trainers when they had been down at the maze. Had Mr Thomson been down there too before breakfast – or last night? Holly gazed at the pattern and suddenly everything slipped into place. The diagram and the maze! Why hadn't she connected the two before?

'Holly!' Miranda pleaded desperately from the doorway.

Holly skipped out of the room just in time. Mrs Billings came bustling out of Peter's room, pushing the vacuum in front of her.

'I heard about you three solving the mystery,' she said, beaming at them. 'Well done!'

'Thanks, Mrs Billings,' the Mystery Kids chorused as the housekeeper made her way along the corridor. They watched her turn into Mr Thomson's room and the vacuum started buzzing again.

'What on earth is wrong with you?' said Peter. 'We nearly got caught!

Holly shook her head. 'I know,' she said. 'But I saw some leaf mould on the carpet and I think I know what's going on.'

Peter and Miranda looked at each other.

'What on earth are you talking about?' said Peter.

Holly bit her lip. 'Come on,' she said. 'I'll show you. It'll be quicker than explaining.'

Holly ran up the stairs to the top floor and across to one of the long windows. Peter and Miranda struggled to keep pace. She slid the window up and scrambled over the sill, racing towards the battlements. Peter and Miranda followed her.

'Look!' she said, pointing towards the maze. 'I'm right; I know I'm right! You must see it.'

She held her breath as Miranda and Peter looked in the direction she was pointing.

'See what?' said Miranda. 'All I see is the maze.'

'Where has Mr Thomson gone?' said Peter.

Holly licked her lips. 'Into the maze,' she said.

'But it's locked,' said Miranda. 'It's been locked for years. The key is lost. And the lock is all rusted up.'

'Maybe he climbed in,' said Peter.

Holly shook her head. 'I don't think so,' she said. 'I think he had a key.'

'Even if he did, it wouldn't work,' said Peter. 'The lock was too rusty.'

'It would work if you oiled the lock,' said Holly.

Peter's mouth dropped open. 'Of course,' he said. 'The missing bottle of oil.'

Holly nodded. 'Remember the state he was in last night when we saw him after dinner?' she said. 'I don't think this is the first time he's been in the maze. But, judging by the way he's all packed up and ready to go, I reckon it'll be the last time.'

'But what is he doing in there?' said Miranda. Then she stopped. 'Are you thinking what I'm thinking?' she said to Holly.

Holly looked at her.

'The Granville Treasure,' they said together.

'It's got to be,' Miranda said, her eyes shining. 'Why else would he be searching like this? It's in the maze.'

Holly nodded. 'It all fits,' she said. 'He knew about the robbery. He's only pretending to be a mystery writer. He attacked Mr Granville. He must be looking for the jewels.'

'But you heard what Mr Granville said. You'd get lost in there,' said Peter.

'Not if you had a ball of string,' said Holly.

Peter looked at her for a moment. Then he clapped a hand to his forehead. 'Of course,' he said. 'Like Theseus and the Minotaur.'

'Who?' said Miranda.

'Theseus,' Peter said. 'It's a Greek legend. He had to go into this maze and kill a monster called the Minotaur. He took a ball of string with him, tied it to the start of the maze and followed it back out after he'd killed the monster.'

'Clever,' said Miranda. 'But it's still risky.'

'What if you have a plan of the maze?' Holly said.

'A plan?' said Peter. 'Like the one on the piece of paper Miranda found?'

Holly pointed at the maze. 'Don't you see?' she said. 'The lighter green bits, the bits where the paths are underneath, they're like the design on that bit of paper. Mr Thomson has a plan of the maze.'

As they watched, there was a movement near the middle of the maze.

'He's in there,' Holly said.

'So what are we doing up here?' said Peter, racing for the window. 'Let's go!'

Holly had to stop Miranda trying to slide down the banisters, she was in such a hurry to get downstairs. They ran out of the house and across the lawns, arriving out of breath at the maze.

Peter tugged at the gate and it swung open on rusty hinges. The lock was smeared with a dark substance.

'Look,' said Miranda rubbing her finger along the keyhole. She lifted her finger to her nose and sniffed. 'It's definitely the bath oil.'

'And look at this,' said Holly.

Tied to the gate was the end of a piece of string.

'He must have been trying to creep out to the maze when Mr Granville came downstairs the other night,' Holly said. 'That's why he had the oil and the string.'

'But Mr Granville disturbed him so he shoved him down the stairs,' said Peter.

'Then we came on the scene and he dropped the oil and string and ran away,' said Miranda.

'That only leaves one question,' said Peter. 'What do we do now?'

The Mystery Kids looked down the deep green tunnel that was the maze. Bits of hedge hung raggedly where they had been chopped away to make a rough path and the ground was deep in dried leaves and newly cut branches.

'We follow the string,' Holly said.

Miranda looked at the chopped off branches. 'You don't think he's got an axe, do you?' she said.

Holly swallowed. 'Would that stop you?' she asked.

Miranda thought for a moment. 'What, just an old axe murderer between me and the Granville Treasure?' she said. 'No way!'

* * *

The string took them twisting and turning through the green tunnels of the maze. Sometimes they seemed to turn back on themselves, sometimes they seemed to go in circles. But always they followed the string.

'Ouch,' said Holly as Peter let a branch whip back in her face.

'Sorry,' said Peter. 'It slipped.'

'That's OK,' said Holly. 'You're getting the worst of it anyway.'

It was true. Peter was having to force his way through at some points. Mr Thomson hadn't cut back much growth and the Mystery Kids had to use hands and arms and feet to shove their way through the overgrown paths.

'What if we get lost?' said Miranda.

Holly looked up. She could see small patches of blue sky between the overgrown branches of the hedges. Underfoot the earth was carpeted with old dead leaves and moss. Their feet didn't make a sound but the hedges on either side shook and vibrated with the force they had to use to get through. Holly hoped it wouldn't give them away.

Peter glanced back and smiled. 'Don't worry about him hearing us,' he said. 'He's having to do this as well.'

Holly smiled back. That thought made her feel a little better. She glanced back at Miranda.

'Just keep to the string and we'll get out again,' she said.

'Can I have that in writing?' Miranda asked.

'Shh,' Holly said and pointed in front of them. Ahead, the light was brighter. 'I think we're coming to the centre.'

Cautiously, the Mystery Kids crept forward until suddenly the hedges gave way to a clear space. Holly gazed through the ragged edges of the hedge.

'There he is,' she mouthed.

Peter and Miranda joined her. Mr Thomson was standing in the middle of a small clearing. In front of him was a pedestal with a stone urn on top of it.

'What's he doing?' whispered Miranda.

Holly shook her head. As they watched, Mr Thomson lifted the top off the urn. It came slowly, stone grating on stone. Then he laid the heavy lid down on the grass and thrust his hand deep into the urn.

Holly held her breath as he brought out a package and laid it carefully on the ground. He took a knife from his pocket and began to cut at the string tying the package together. It seemed to be wrapped in material of some kind. They watched as he carefully unrolled the material and Holly couldn't help gasping as she saw what was in the package.

'The jewels!' breathed Miranda.

Holly watched as Mr Thomson held up a necklace and gazed at it greedily. She recognised it. It was the necklace that hung round the neck of the Honorable Amelia Granville in the portrait at the top of the stairs.

'The Granville Treasure,' Peter whispered. 'We were right! It's the missing jewels!'

'We've found them,' said Miranda, her face alight.

Holly looked at the others. 'Maybe,' she said. 'But we haven't got them – Thomson has. So what do we do about that?'

The trap

Thomson began to thrust handfuls of jewels into his pockets.

'Quick,' said Peter. 'He'll be leaving in a moment. He'll catch us.'

'I don't understand this,' said Miranda. 'Thomson can't be the thief. The thief died in prison.'

'But Thomson obviously knew where the thief hid the jewels,' Peter said.

'How?' said Miranda.

Holly bit her lip. 'That isn't important right now,' she said. 'We've got to stop him.'

She looked at Thomson. How could they stop him getting away with the jewels while they got help?

'But what can we do?' Miranda said. 'I mean I know we're three against one, but he's got a knife.'

'And he's already attacked Mr Granville,' Peter added. 'I don't fancy tackling him.'

'But we can't just let him escape,' said Holly.

Peter's face lit up. 'We don't have to,' he said. 'Look!'

The girls looked where he was pointing. There, lying on a stone bench near the edge of the clearing was the ball of string and the plan of the maze.

Holly, Peter and Miranda peered through the hedge. Thomson was picking up the lid of the stone urn. The string and the plan lay on the bench just a few metres away. It would only take a moment to dart out into the open, pick them up then run for cover again. It could be done – if only Thomson didn't turn round.

'Quick!' said Holly. 'While he's putting the lid back.'

Peter waited until Thomson had grasped the lid with both hands and was lifting it towards the urn. Then he crept out from behind the hedge, reached over and picked up the ball of string. Holly saw Thomson's head turn slightly. Peter froze where he was.

'Don't turn round,' Holly pleaded under her breath. Peter was right out in the open.

Thomson shook his head and continued to lift the stone lid. Holly's breath came out in a little sigh.

Then Peter was moving again. His feet made barely a sound on the cushion of dead leaves. He reached out and picked up the diagram.

Holly held her breath as he darted back to them.

'Got it,' he said as he reached cover again.

'Now what?' said Miranda.

'Now we follow the string back,' said Holly. 'But we roll it up as we go.'

'And trap Thomson in the maze while we go for help,' Miranda said. 'That is brilliant!'

There was the sound of stone grating on stone and Peter peered round the hedge. 'Quick,' he said. 'Thomson's coming!'

Holly grabbed the string and began to run, rolling it up as she went. But she was running faster than she could roll and the string was being left behind in a big loop. If Thomson caught up with them he would be able to pick up the trail of the string.

'Never mind rolling it, just haul it in,' Peter yelled.

Behind them they heard a roar and Thomson's voice.

'Who's there?' he shouted. 'What are you doing?'

Holly grabbed handfuls of string as best she could. She looked back. She could see the hedge shaking where Thomson was crashing around, looking for the way out.

'Quick!' said Peter. 'Let's get out of here.'

But that was easier said than done. The string caught in the ragged hedges as they ran and fell tangled at their feet, threatening to trip them up.

The Mystery Kids ran on, twisting and turning through the paths of the maze, doubling back on themselves, losing all sense of direction but following the string, their lifeline to the outside world. Branches scratched their faces and arms and roots seemed to spring out to trip them up but they kept doggedly on. All the time, Thomson kept after them.

Peter stopped suddenly and dropped to his knees, dragging the girls down beside him.

'Shh,' he said. 'He's coming this way. If he sees us we've had it!'

Holly and Miranda crouched close under the hedge. The string stretched in front of them, showing the way out. Great piles of it lay tangled at their feet but they couldn't leave it behind. And they hadn't anything to cut it with.

Holly looked back at the gap at the end of the alleyway. She could hear Thomson coming nearer and nearer. If he didn't turn down this path, they might be all right.

All at once the hedge behind them began to shake wildly and Holly jumped as she heard Thomson's voice.

'It's you kids; I know it is!' he roared. 'Where are you?'

His voice sounded as if it was right in her ear. Then she realised he was in the next alleyway. He was just on the other side of the hedge from them.

She looked at Peter and Miranda. Peter put his finger to his lips. He was right. They had to stay absolutely still or Thomson would know where they were. Holly looked at the hedge and swallowed. Could Thomson crash through it?

They heard him moving away but still the three crouched where they were, their eyes on the gap at the end of the alleyway. Suddenly Thomson rushed past the opening and down another path. They heard his voice receding.

'Now!' Peter said. Holly and Miranda leapt to their feet and ran, never daring to stop. In and out they went, twisting and turning through the maze. Behind them they could hear Thomson crashing about.

At last there was a glimmer of light at the end of the path.

'Look!' said Miranda, breathless from running. 'There's the gate. We've done it!'

The Mystery Kids shot out of the maze. Holly threw the string to the ground and the three of them raced for the house.

'Get Mr Granville!' Peter yelled. 'I'm going to ring the police!'

Holly and Miranda found the Granvilles in the kitchens with Mark.

'Where have you been?' Mrs Granville said. 'You look a mess!'

'Quick!' said Holly. 'You've got to come at once! It's Thomson. We've got him. He's in the maze with the Granville Treasure!'

Mrs Granville looked at her and stopped drying the plate she was holding.

'What?' she said to Holly.

'The Granville Treasure?' Mr Granville said. 'You mean you've found it?'

Holly nodded and Miranda grabbed Mr Granville's arm. 'Peter has gone to phone the police,' she said. 'But we've got to get back to the maze. Thomson might escape! He might find the way out!'

Mr and Mrs Granville looked at each other. But Mark was already halfway out of the kitchen and heading for the door to the great hall.

'Explanations can wait,' Mrs Granville said to her husband. 'I'll find Peter and talk to the police.'

Mr Granville ran a hand through his hair. 'You three are something else,' he said. 'I don't know what you've been up to but let's get down there!'

Then they were out of the house. Mr Granville raced ahead, his long legs covering the ground at a sprint. Holly could see that Mark was already halfway to the maze.

'Listen to Thomson,' Miranda said as they ran down the front steps of the house. 'You can hear him yelling from here!'

Behind them, bedroom windows began to shoot up and heads poked out.

'What's going on down there?' Mrs Partridge called from her bedroom window.

Miss Finch and the Martins were piling luggage into a taxi on the driveway but Holly and Miranda swept on past, pounding across the lawn. The yells from the maze were getting louder.

By now Mr Granville and Mark had reached the entrance gate. Even if Thomson did manage to get out of the maze now those two could deal with him. Mr Granville turned to Holly and Miranda as they caught up with him.

'Did you actually see the treasure?' he said.

Holly nodded. 'Some of it,' she said breathlessly. 'I saw the necklace that the Honourable

Amelia Granville is wearing in that portrait on the top landing.'

Mr Granville smiled. 'If you're right about this, we won't have to sell the house.'

'Did you hear that?' said Holly as a police siren sounded.

The yelling from inside the maze stopped suddenly.

Miranda nodded. 'I think Thomson heard it too,' she said.

Holly looked at Mr Granville. He was frowning.

'What's the matter?' she said.

'I'm just trying to remember the way into the maze,' he said. 'I never was very much good at getting in and out of there and its been overgrown for years.'

'Don't worry about that,' Holly said. 'We've got a plan.' She held out the diagram. 'We pinched it from Thomson.'

'And a ball of string just to be on the safe side,' Miranda said. She looked at the sorry pile of tangled string on the ground by the gate. 'At least, it used to be a ball of string,' she said.

There was a crunching of car tyres on the

gravel of the drive and Mrs Granville came out of the front door to meet the police car. Peter was with her.

Doors slammed as three policemen got out of the car and started walking towards the maze. Mr Granville looked at Holly and Miranda.

'I don't know where to start explaining all this to the police,' he said.

'Don't worry,' said Holly. 'I'm sure Peter's told them all about it.'

'I'm Sergeant Perkins,' said the policeman in front. He looked at Peter. 'This young man has been telling us quite a story.'

Mr Granville nodded. 'I know it's hard to believe, sergeant,' he said. 'It all started rather a long time ago.'

Sergeant Perkins smiled. 'No need to explain, Mr Granville,' he said. 'I was on the case when those jewels were stolen.'

Mr Granville looked surprised.

Sergeant Perkins nodded. 'Of course I was just a youngster at the time,' he said. 'I always wondered what happened to them.'

'So did I, sergeant,' Mr Granville said. 'And

thanks to these three, it looks as if we've found them.'

A sudden thought occurred to Holly. 'Oh, no!' she said. 'Thomson heard the police car. What if he hides the jewels again somewhere in the maze?'

But just at that moment Thomson's voice came loud and clear.

'Get me out of here,' he yelled.

Sergeant Perkins grinned. 'I reckon Thomson has other things on his mind, don't you?' he said. He turned to the two young policemen with him and handed them the map and the end of the tangle of string. 'Get in there,' he ordered, 'and don't lose hold of that string or we'll never get you out.'

The two policeman looked at each other and dived into the maze.

Holly could hear them calling to Thomson, trying to locate him. After what seemed like an age one of the policemen shouted back.

'Got him, Sarge!'

Thomson looked pretty sorry for himself when the policemen eventually led him out. He still had the packet of jewels on him.

'We'll need you to check it over, Mr

Granville,' Sergeant Perkins said. 'See if it's all there.'

Mr Granville tipped the package and the jewels spilled out, sparkling in the sunlight.

Thomson looked at the Mystery Kids. 'All those years they were there waiting and you have to interfere,' he said.

'But how did you know they were there?' said Holly.

'I shared a cell with Palmer.' Thomson sneered. 'He knew he was dying so he gave me the key of the maze and the map and told me where he had stashed the stuff.'

'You mean you were in prison too?' said Miranda.

Thomson laughed unpleasantly. 'You don't really think I write mystery stories, do you?' he said.

'As a matter of fact, no,' Miranda said loftily. 'You didn't know anything about mystery writers.'

'Coming on the weekend was just an excuse,' Peter said.

'So that you could look for the jewels without anybody being suspicious,' said Holly.

'Clever!' Miranda said. 'I mean everybody

is supposed to be snooping around on a mystery weekend, aren't they?'

'As far as we're concerned, you can come here and snoop any time you like,' Mr Granville said.

'Maybe we'll change our name to Super-snoops,' Miranda said.

Holly gave her a look. 'No way,' she said. 'It's the Mystery Kids for ever!'

Another Hodder Children's book

Fiona Kelly

BLACKMAIL!
THE MYSTERY KIDS 7

Is their hero really a thief?

A chance to meet the actor who plays Secret Agent John Raven on TV – it's what the Mystery Kids always wanted!

But John Raven isn't too polite when they approach him in the park. So the three friends follow him – and what they see him do gives them a *big* surprise.

Is the Mystery Kids' hero up to no good?

Fiona Kelly

WRONG NUMBER
THE MYSTERY KIDS 9

Something suspicious on the line . . .

The Mystery Kids are on the trail of stolen cars. At first it's a bit of fun – background information for an article in their school magazine.

Then they get a suspicious wrong-number phone call about a local garage.

And it's clear that *someone* at the garage is up to no good!